FOUR SISTERS

IN

PARIS

Marty Almquist

This is a work of fiction. While, as in all fiction, the literary perceptions and insights are based on experience, all names, characters, places, and events either are products of the author's imagination or are used fictitiously.

ISBN-13: 978-0-9852624-0-2

ACKNOWLEDGMENTS

This is a story about sisters so my first thank you has to be to my sisters (and friends) who inspired me to write this. Though the story itself is entirely fictional, the support I get from them is absolutely real. And to Mom, who showed us the way by example.

The writing of this story has been a fun adventure, and I want to thank Nellie Sabin, a remarkable editor and friend. A big thanks also to Jan Day Gravel for introducing me to Nellie and to my special support group—you know who you are. Thanks also to Rosalia Diaz and Cassa Leonard for their incredible creative genius and amazing book cover art. And thanks to Sharon Rogolsky who did a wonderful job copy editing.

Finally, thanks to the folks at A La Carte Maps (www.alacartemaps.com) who let me use their map of Paris to show where the sisters' adventures took them.

I hope this story inspires you to go and visit Paris for yourself.

To Peter, who is my soul mate

Avenue de Villiers

Boulevard des Batignolles

de Clichy

Rue Blanche

Rue d'Amsterdam

N
W E
S

Boulevard de Courcelles

Boulevard Malesherbes

Rue de

Boulevard Haussman

Avenue Friedland

Madeleine

c de Triomphe

Avenue Kléber

Avenue d'Iéna

Avenue Marceau

Avenue des Champs-Élysées

Boulevard des Italiens

Opéra

Day 5
Grand Palais
(Marie Antoinette Exhibit)

Jardin des Tuile

Pont Alexandre III

Voie sur Berge Rive Gauche

Avenue Rapp

Tour Eiffel

Avenue Bosquet

Musée d'Orsay

Qua

Day 4
Impressionist
paintings

Saint Sulpi

Boulevard Raspail

Saint Germain

Avenue de Breteuil

Boulevard Garibaldi

Rue de Sèvres

Avenue du Maine

Jardin du Lux

Rue Lecourbe

Rue de Vaugirard

Boulevard Pasteur

Boulevard Montparnasse

Boulevar

Boulevard de la Chapelle

Day 3
Marché Aux Puces
Flea Market

Rue de Faubourg Saint-Denis

Canal St Martin

Avenue

Rue La Fayette

udun

Boulevard de Magenta

Rue de Belleville

Rue Réaumur

Avenue de la République

Rue de Turbigo

Boulevard de Sébastopol

Rue Beaubourg

Boulevard Voltaire

Louvre

Day 1
Carol's
favorite
place

Rue de Rivoli

Voie Georges Pompidou

Hôtel de Ville

Place des Vosges

ais

Notre Dame

Musée de Cluny

Boulevard Henri IV

Bastille

Rue du Fau

Boulevard Saint-Germain

Voie Georges Pompidou

Panthéon

Avenue Ledru-Rollin

Day 2
Latin Quarter
(shopping
boutique)

Rue Monge

Gare d'Austerlitz
Ⓜ

Quai d'Austerlitz

Prologue

She was alone. The office was quiet, dark, and still. If she listened hard enough, she could hear the gentle buzz of the light overhead, its bulb dimmed by time and dust. Wearily she rubbed her eyes and looked back down at the figures in front of her. By blinking she could get them into focus, but it did nothing to make them more appealing. She was in trouble and she knew it. The two newest contracts were still not signed by the clients (the bill for the dinner to persuade them was on the top of the pile), the copier was broken... again... and now she was worried about Andrew. He said he had great connections and was going to double their client base, but all she'd seen so far were more bills. Did he really know the right people at the two new hotels? Getting their insurance business would mean monthly retainers that would cover the basic bills... a huge step up from the current paycheck-to-paycheck lifestyle for them and their few employees.

Who could she talk to about this? No one local, that was for sure. Too small a community and any hint of concern on her part would give the hotels the excuse they needed to choose someone else. Maybe she could talk to Margot, Sophie and Carol when she saw them? That path had its own complications, but it might be the lesser of two evils.

She stood, gently massaging her lower back in a vain effort to remove the permanent ache. If she ever had any extra money, she'd do that therapy that was recommended after her physical two years ago. Well, she could at least take a walk around the office to clear her brain and grab a Diet Coke out of the fridge. Moving around the desk, she paused at the doorway, letting her eyes adjust to the dimness beyond. The emergency lighting meant it was not completely dark and she worked her way down the hallway, stopping outside Andrew's office. She paused, feeling like an intruder, but shook off the feeling and opened the door. She realized she hadn't been in it since his first week—generally their conversations were limited to the weekly sales meeting in the conference room or a quick update in the small kitchen if their paths crossed.

She reached over to turn on the lamp that sat at one corner of the desk, noting with a shake of her head that it was emblazoned with his beloved Redskins' trademark. Who knew why he loved a team on the other side of the country? His desk was neat, with two small piles stacked on one side. Idly she picked up one of the stacks and glanced down at the paper on top. It was a bill for four tickets to the latest Cirque de Soleil show. She was appalled at the price, though she knew the tickets were very hard to get. She fervently hoped they were for a client. Circling the room, she came to the small leather sofa that he'd brought in during his second week and sank down onto it, continuing to leaf through the stack she'd picked up. Another bill for show tickets, then bills for lunches each day this week at high-end restaurants. Turning them over, she could see names written on the back in his sprawl, denoting the clients he had taken each time. Well, at least it *looked* like business development. Relieved, she finished her review and, with a small grimace, pushed herself off of the sofa.

Out of the corner of her eye, she saw something bright and turned back to see what had caught her attention. There, just at the edge of the far cushion. Something red? Setting the stack of papers back onto the desk where she'd found them, she returned to the couch and reached for the speck of red. Pulling on it revealed a small pair of bright red, lace panties. Now *that* was definitely *not* related to business development—at least not any business that she wanted to know about. She slumped back onto the sofa, overwhelmed by this newest evidence of his stupidity that added itself mercilessly to her growing mountain of worries. The resultant wave of despair threatened to crush her.

What in the *hell* was she going to do??

Chapter 1. Margot

I had my routine down. Arriving at the airport three hours in advance of the 6:00 p.m. flight, I checked my bag, passed through security, and headed to the Firkin, the bar near the gate, for a burger and a beer. Past experience had taught me that eating my meal here at the airport meant I could go right to sleep once I was on board. We would land in Paris at 6:30 in the morning, and though my normal routine was to catch the bus and arrive at the apartment about 8:30, this time I would be waiting at the airport for my sisters to arrive.

I chose a bar stool and got out my notebook to think about what the schedule should be for the next five days. After ordering a cheeseburger and a Stella, I stared at the blank page. How much should I plan? For the first time in a long time, I would be with all my sisters—sisters I'd been very close to growing up, but sisters I didn't really know any more. Amy I'd seen recently, but it had been years since I'd seen Sophie or Carol. There would be a lot of catching up to do.

Amy, Sophie, Carol, and me, the Four Mitchell Sisters. With only six years between the four of us, we'd been a force to be reckoned with. All four smart, full of energy, and driven by ambition to be "somebody" someday—somebody who wasn't scraping along paycheck to paycheck, considering a $4.00 latte a forbidden treat. Dad had done his best, but working at the post office was not a high-paying job, and Mom's job at the phone company added just enough to the family income to make sure we never went hungry and that we had a roof over our heads. College had been possible only with loans, scholarships, and lots of campus and summer jobs, but we had all gotten through and into the big wide world.

Those early years when we were all at home had been noisy and full of debate and conversation, our voices sometimes raised in argument and sometimes joyful in shared success. Sophie, being the oldest, had always been sure that she was right and that she needed to be in control. Her take-charge disposition now served her well in her job as director of west coast operations for R.L. Smith, one of the top five accounting firms. Carol, less than a year younger, was the quiet peacemaker of the group. She had opinions, but you had to ask for them directly rather than expect that she would voice them. I came along two years after Carol, and then there had been three full years before Amy came along. From the first, she was the rowdiest and most adventurous of us all. The loudest clashes came when Amy's stubbornness collided with Sophie's lofty assumption that she was "obviously correct." Carol and I had hovered between the two, though I tended to side with Amy on most issues and was always ready to join her wild and crazy schemes.

My burger arrived but I was lost in thought. Those partying days now seemed a lifetime ago. How had we drifted apart? Looking back, I could see that the first step for Sophie, Carol and me had been when we each left for college. Amy, in typical fashion, had taken a less direct route, with some twists and turns before she settled down. She had finally gotten her degree, but unlike the rest of us, she had chosen to stay near Mom and Dad.

After that first separation, I took an additional step away by spending my junior year in Paris. Money was tight and plane flights were prohibitively expensive, so there were no trips home. That ten months completely on my own were exhilarating, frustrating, challenging, and yet also inspiring, and by the end of my stay, I knew that Paris and its magic would be a part of me forever.

My boyfriend Paul came to visit after his graduation and we got engaged during our two-month backpacking trip.

After college, jobs took us to completely different parts of the U.S. with Sophie moving to Salt Lake City, Carol to Chicago, and I to Virginia. Working full-time and starting families became our new priorities.

During Christmas vacations for the first years of our marriage, Paul and I traveled back to see both sets of parents, but when our two boys came along—first Mark, and then Carl three years later—we felt we needed to be at home so Santa could "find" us. Our new pattern became a trip west every other year, and we alternated between the two sets of grandparents. When the boys were young, we also made the effort to visit Carol and Sophie and their families regularly, but that got more and more difficult as everyone's schedules filled with sports commitments and school activities, and there was never enough vacation time. Paul and I also wanted to introduce the boys to a wide variety of places and cultures and we treasured our brief trips to Europe. We wanted them to understand and love other languages and ways of life.

For my sisters, coming to visit us was just as complicated. Sophie traveled so much for her job that she preferred staying close to home when possible. Like us, she and Roger had two boys, Bobby and Jeremy, both very active in sports, so she limited her travel schedule during football and soccer seasons.

Carol also had two kids, and her job pressure was not one of travel but of responsibility. She never felt she could be away for long.

The combination of all of these pressures in all of our lives meant that, eventually, the trips ended and our communication with each other was reduced to phone calls, e-mails, and Christmas cards. It wasn't a good substitute.

We did see Amy whenever we visited Mom and Dad, so at least I felt I had an ongoing relationship with her.

The deeper discussions that my sisters and I used to have about relationships and life events didn't translate well to hurried telephone calls. We talked less and less, and therefore knew less and less about each other's daily lives. Our conversations felt more and more shallow. Now, when we did talk on the phone, I sometimes felt uncomfortable. Words became stilted and there were awkward gaps of silence. These days I sent e-mails to my sisters only when there was something that I thought they would find fun or amusing, and those e-mails didn't even require an answer.

Turning fifty this year had filled me with a sense of time running away. In looking at my life and my relationships, I realized I needed deep connections with people I loved and trusted, for my own well-being. The friends we'd made in Virginia weren't enough. I interacted with plenty of people every day because of my job in real estate, but although my phone was filled with contact numbers, there was no one I wanted to call. I made a promise to myself that I would use this fiftieth year to see all of my family.

The reconnection with my sisters came in a very different way than I had hoped. Mom had called in October, saying that she had colon cancer and would need to undergo surgery and a series of chemotherapy treatments. That started a round of e-mails and phone conversations as we all went into support mode. After her surgery, we took turns helping her through the chemo weekends and, just as importantly, keeping Dad company. He simply could not understand that his wife of fifty years, who had always taken care of him, was now in need of care herself. Our presence was an obvious relief to him and helped him adjust. Gradually he began to take over many of the daily tasks, like cleaning and cooking, that our mother had always managed for him.

We still did not get physical time together since our visits didn't overlap, but we were in constant contact by phone and e-mail, sharing our concerns about both parents. The frequent conversations also gave us the chance to get advice from each other on problems we each faced at home in our own "mom" roles.

When we all felt comfortable that our mother was on the road to recovery, we decided that a weekend reconnecting as sisters would be a great way to celebrate. After much e-mail traffic, we finally came up with the date: an extended weekend in May that worked for everyone.

The next tough decision was where. Nothing seemed right. It was already getting too hot in the South or West in May, and yet it wasn't quite warm enough to go up North.

That's when I thought about Paris. Five years before, Paul and I had bought a small two-bedroom apartment on the Right Bank, within easy walking distance of Notre Dame and the Marais area. I was hesitant to suggest it as a possible destination because I knew that a trip to Europe would be viewed by everyone as a big commitment, and that most spouses would react much more favorably to something simpler and cheaper, like a "girls' trip to the beach." After extensive discussions among the various couples, I was thrilled that all three sisters succeeded in persuading their families that Paris could work. After all, the apartment would make the trip more affordable, and the opportunity for us all to be in the same place at the same time might not come again.

Looking at my watch, I realized that I had made no progress on creating an itinerary. I loved the idea of sharing this place with my sisters, but I was suddenly struck by uncertainty. I didn't know these women anymore. Would we still find things to laugh about, would we want to share stories of our lives? I wouldn't know until we spent some time together. Moreover, none of my sisters had ever been to Paris. Would I be an adequate hostess and tour guide? I wanted everyone to have a wonderful time—especially since they were coming so far and braving the unknown.

Each sister had roadblocks to overcome to take this trip. Sophie's husband was very possessive of both her and her time. When her career began to skyrocket, and it became obvious that to advance she would have to move every few years, Roger chose to quit his job, and he had been a "house husband" ever since. The situation seemed to work well for both of them and for their two sons, who as teenagers now loved having a father available to attend all their various football and soccer games. Roger had finally been convinced that this trip was an important reconnection for all the sisters, and he was grudgingly "letting" Sophie go.

Carol's issue was primarily her job. She worked at a large non-profit that did government research, running the day-to-day operations and spearheading their fundraising efforts. She was a critical part of the daily decision-making process and she feared her staff would panic at having to manage on their own. Secretly I wondered whether Carol was more worried about her own absence from the office than her team was. But then again she could always find something to worry about. Carol's husband, George, was a consultant of some sort, and though I wasn't sure exactly what he did, my impression was that he had enough flexibility to be the full-time caretaker of their teenagers, Gwen and Brian, for a short period of time.

Amy had started her own insurance claims processing company two years ago and seemed buried by the multitude of responsibilities that go with being an entrepreneur. Being divorced meant that she also had half-time custody of her 15-year-old son, and I knew she found juggling the two sides of her life overwhelming at times. How could she fit in a trip for five days? But in the end I had persuaded her that Mom's recent cancer scare was a reminder of the need for family. That seemed to be the argument she needed, because she had e-mailed me soon after that discussion to say she'd made her reservation.

Now, sitting here waiting for my flight, it was hitting me that the idea and dream would soon become a reality. I would find out whether my instincts about this trip had been good or not.

And so, back to the blank page of my notebook. I wanted to create a list of things to do, since I was the only one with any knowledge of the city, but I didn't want my sisters to feel that I had planned every second of the trip.

Shaking my head, I closed the notebook. Knowing the personalities that were coming together, there would be plenty of discussion, which would eventually lead to decisions, so there was no need for me to do anything further. I paid my bill and, with a suddenly rapid heartbeat, headed to the gate to wait for the boarding call.

Chapter 2. Sophie

Sophie ran through her mental travel checklist, honed from so many business trips, but this time her confidence in that list was lacking. This trip was for pleasure; she was going to a city she'd never seen, and she would be with sisters she had not spent time with in years. She was feeling distinctly out of her element, which added to her level of stress. She reminded herself they were sisters, not strangers, but she knew it wasn't that simple. Though she was sure they would all settle in quickly, she felt it was important to make the right first impression.

What clothes should she pack? The Internet told her that May in Paris generally included some rain and temperatures in the sixties. Margot had said not to look "too American." What was that supposed to mean? No fanny pack or baseball cap? Sophie wouldn't have considered either of those anyway. She already had versatile and comfortable travel clothes. She decided to pack dark pants, comfortable shoes for walking, several loose-fitting tops, a sweater for cooler evenings, and one skirt in case they decided to do something more formal.

She began to pull out clothes from the closet and realized with a smile that some were going to be too big. The polite term used to describe her when she was young had been "big-boned." (She had certainly heard plenty of other terms that she would rather not remember.) Going away to college had been a way to escape those terms and the people who had used them. Living on her own after college, she had her first epiphany. She realized she did not have to be ashamed because she was not a size eight like Margot. In the working world, her confidence continued to grow as her talents were recognized and rewarded with rapid promotions. Those promotions led to travel throughout the U.S., which in turn introduced her to an ever-growing variety of delicious food. It was harder and harder to balance what she considered one of life's greatest pleasures—eating fabulous, fresh, local dishes— with her desire to be slimmer.

That's when she had her second epiphany. She needed to stop trying different diets and instead change the way she thought about food. Also, her attitude about exercise needed improving. Sophie was a strong, confident person in all other aspects in her life, and she told herself that she simply needed to apply her analytical skills to this "problem" just like any other she might encounter. So desserts, bread, and cheese continued to be a part of her life, but in moderation. Every day, each thing she ate or drank she judged as worthy or not worthy. If worthy, she ate or drank it and enjoyed every bite. If not worthy (say, dessert at a business function that had been made for 200 people and frankly tasted like sawdust), she said "no thank you" and had a cup of coffee instead. Eventually she realized how often eating was actually an emotional response rather than a physical need. Now it was second nature to ask herself two questions when faced with something to eat: first, was it worth it? And second, what else had she already eaten that day? After that it was simply a matter of finding an exercise routine she could follow at home and on the road.

After creating several piles of possible clothing choices, she went to get a cup of coffee. She always found that, if she gave herself a break while packing, it was easier to remove unnecessary items—plus she also often remembered some critical item that she had forgotten. Passing the mirror on her bureau, she paused a moment, giving herself a critical once-over. Five feet nine inches tall, and her posture was still good. Her light brown hair was sprinkled with gray and, frankly, in need of some new highlights. Pushing her hair behind one ear reminded her that it was getting thinner, too. She knew that stress was one of the reasons, so she was trying to learn to be more relaxed, but it just wasn't her nature. Overall her face still seemed relatively unlined. "Not bad for an old lady," she thought, and continued on into the kitchen.

Sitting with her steaming cup, enjoying the late afternoon sun filtering in, she realized how nervous she really was about this trip. She'd traveled a great deal, but never abroad. She didn't speak French. She didn't know Paris. She had left the planning up to Margot, which meant giving up any sense of control. Sophie preferred plotting out each step of her life, at work and at home, and following the path thus created in an organized way. She did *not* care for unknowns and surprises. Roger had tried giving her a surprise birthday party one time and learned from that experience that "surprise" was not a positive thing to Sophie's way of thinking, ever. When she had walked unsuspectingly into a restaurant filled with friends and family, she did not feel jolly—she felt ambushed. And yet here she was, about to put herself into a situation that would be full of uncertainty and surprises. That was, pure and simple, a hard thing for her to do.

Could she trust Margot to plan a successful trip? She paused for a moment to think about that. Growing up, they had all depended on each other. But had she totally trusted Margot even then? For Sophie, high school had been full of insecurity and unhappiness. Her sisters had been her only allies during those awful years, but in her skin-tight jeans with her wild boyfriends, Margot had not always been understanding or sympathetic. Sophie remembered many lonely Saturday nights, when Margot would stumble in from another of her parties, stinking of alcohol and giggling about her latest adventures. After both were out of college and living on their own, the two of them had become much closer, but Sophie was reminded that her goal in choosing a college had been to get as far away as possible, emotionally as well as physically, from her unhappy teenage social life. It had been the first in a series of moves to different parts of the country that ultimately distanced her from her family support network.

How well did she know Margot anymore? Certainly there had been lots more conversation over the stressful months of their mother's illness. Sophie had always thought of her family as close, but had to admit that before all this recent mom-related activity, she couldn't remember the last meaningful conversation she'd had with any of her sisters or her parents. She sent cards for birthdays and holidays, and called them sporadically to catch up in a general way, but those conversations couldn't even begin to cover all that happened each week in a life that she herself found overwhelming.

She found it particularly difficult to talk to her mother, whose life had followed such a different path. The simplest description of an episode at work required a major amount of background information to make it meaningful. It was even more difficult for her mother to understand that her responsibilities often spilled over into the evenings, with her service on community boards, and social commitments with employees and her peers in the business community. Her connections with her employees and their spouses outside of work helped make her a beloved manager, and that in turn led to the awards she won each year.

She loved it all, and didn't begrudge a single minute —but she realized that her life had tightened into an ever-smaller circle, until the only people she really talked to were her own immediate family and her friends through work. The call from Margot had started her brain churning through old memories, and she kept finding good ones that usually centered on her sisters and the silly, fun times they'd shared. She allowed herself to remember the cooking, the banter, the conversations whispered long after the lights were out. She began to feel eager to discover what kinds of women her sisters had become, and maybe even to find a piece of herself that she had left behind.

The more Sophie recalled, the more she realized she missed those teasing, candid, no-holds-barred conversations that used to be so much a part of her life. She couldn't remember the last time she had really let loose in a conversation with anyone besides Roger. Joan, her best friend at work, had been at R.L. Smith almost as long as she had, and was certainly one of the few people she felt she could relax with, but there was always a small piece of reserve that warned, "This is someone you work with—better not be too honest, or say too much. You never know when it might come back to haunt you."

Well, enough introspection. Time to get back to packing. Margot had insisted that she bring just one bag, saying, "There are lots of stairs in the metro system and very few escalators or elevators, so be sure you can easily carry whatever you bring." Smiling, she walked back up the stairs to put everything in her "one bag." She pulled out her cosmetic kit and threw in her face lotion and mascara. She had never really felt comfortable with cosmetics and didn't feel like she knew how to use them. Now that she had passed the big half-century mark, maybe she should treat herself and go to a spa and take a make-up class. She loved manicures and pedicures, but had just never learned to use much in the way of makeup. Maybe her sisters would have pointers to share. Who knew what she might learn on this trip?

Chapter 3. Amy

"Mom, where are my basketball sneakers?" Josh bellowed from the front door.

"Where you left them when you came in last night—next to the TV," Amy answered as she came out into the hallway. She smiled at her son, amazed as always at how tall he was for age fifteen and how much he looked like his father.

"Mom, I've got practice after school so I'll catch the late bus."

"Sounds good.   I figured we'd have homemade stir-fry. How does that sound?"

"Awesome." He opened the door. "See ya later."

Amy started toward him. "Wait! Don't I get a kiss?"

Josh bent his head, reluctantly, so she could peck his cheek and darted out the door.

Amy continued into the kitchen and grabbed a soda out of the fridge. Never a fan of coffee or hot tea, she started her mornings with a soda for her caffeine fix. At the office they always gave her a hard time about it, but she was by nature a very warm-blooded person and had never cared for hot drinks.

Amy carried the soda back to her room to survey her packing progress. Margot had said to pack everything in one bag. She could do that. So far she had some tops she'd picked up at Target yesterday, a couple of pairs of jeans, and comfortable shoes. She smiled as she remembered Margot's admonition not to look "too American." She had never been to France, but she was pretty sure the usual *mademoiselle* was not a generously proportioned 5'8" with blue eyes and strawberry blond hair.

Amy put the last few clothes in her luggage, and then squeezed in her large bag of cosmetics. She had enough creams and lotions for all four sisters, as well as four different eye shadow collections, three colors of lipstick, and every variety of hair product. "After all," she thought to herself, "it's all about choices, right?"

Done! Setting the bag at the foot of her bed, she went to sit on the loveseat in the corner, her favorite thinking spot. She had a few minutes left before work. Settling into the big, soft cushions, she thought about the upcoming trip. This would be a very interesting long weekend, watching everyone get reacquainted in person.

Where had the time gone? She'd been divorced almost four years. Hard to believe. Jim was an incredibly nice guy, but not a great businessman. They were already growing apart when Josh had come along, and then everything had gotten even more complicated. Jim seemed less and less able to cope with the ever-increasing responsibilities in their lives, especially anything involving parenthood, until one night he did something that Amy simply couldn't forgive.

The divorce left her with the house—her parents helped her pay Jim for his share—and half-time custody of Josh. Knowing she needed to increase her income, she had approached Melinda, her best friend at her most recent job, and suggested they take their knowledge of the insurance business and their contacts and start their own company. Doing so had been more complicated and more stressful than Amy had ever imagined, but the business had begun to pick up. Just at the end of last year she felt things were finally moving in the right direction.

In January they had added a third partner, Andrew, who spoke with confidence about his many connections to companies who would want their services. Melinda agreed they needed a partner, but it was Amy who had pushed for Andrew. She was beginning to wish she had waited longer. Time would tell if he could deliver what he'd promised, but he had her worried. Just last month she had overheard Andrew boasting about his expensive taste in business lunches to their new, pretty receptionist. Amy had been too busy to look closely at his expense receipts, assuming Andrew would behave sensibly. Now she was learning that an entrepreneur and small business owner could not afford to assume anything. Upon closer review, Andrew's expenses were *way* out of line. She would have to speak to him after she returned.

Andrew's resume listed great contacts and past experience, and his previous employer was happy to speak favorably of him, but she was starting to wonder whether he was going to be an asset or a liability. Did his previous employer "pass the trash"? According to his resume, Andrew's last two jobs had been in Reno, so Amy had quietly talked to a friend of hers there and had asked him to see what he could find out. She expected to hear from him any minute. She was glad there would be Internet access at the apartment in Paris.

Pushing concerns about her company to the back of her mind, Amy thought instead about the trip. She was so excited! She loved to travel, but had not had the money or time these last few years to do so. Margot's call could not have been better timed. With her sixty- to seventy-hour work weeks, Amy needed a break. She knew she didn't really have the money for this trip, but she also knew that she was burned out and had lost confidence in herself and her recent decisions. Melinda had pushed her to go, saying the time away from the daily grind might help Amy bring back some fresh ideas. She could leave the day-to-day operations in Melinda's capable hands, and she would have her Blackberry for issues that might need her input.

Amy would be taking two flights, one to Chicago tomorrow morning, then a second at 5:30 p.m. from Chicago to Paris. By sheer luck, she and Carol would be on the same flight out of Chicago. It would be great to be flying together! She and Carol could get caught up a little before meeting everyone else at the airport. Margot had said that her flight got in first, at 6:30 a.m., and that she would meet them when they got to baggage claim. Amy and Carol would arrive at 8:45 a.m. and Sophie at 9:45 a.m. She was glad that Margot had agreed to wait for them instead of making them find their own way from the airport to the apartment. Speaking no French, Amy was happy to let Margot take charge. As the baby of the family, she generally let one of her older sisters take the lead.

What else did she need to arrange today? Josh didn't get along with Jim's new wife, so she had asked her friend Jeannie to come stay at the house. Jeannie was a stay-at-home mom with a four-year-old, Jason. Jeannie's husband had left the day she told him of Jason's upcoming arrival, so she and Jason lived in a tiny apartment in a building owned by her parents. She was always up for house-sitting jobs as a way to give Jason more space to run around. They would be arriving later to spend the night. For Jeannie, adding Josh to the general chaos of her daily life wasn't difficult because she had nieces and nephews Josh's age and often acted as a second mother to them. She knew the way their schedules worked and was wise to the food, electronics, and daily crises of a teen's life. Amy had written out Josh's basketball schedule and would just pray for no injuries. Jeannie had her cell number—Amy had paid the fee to make sure it would work in Europe—and the phone number at the apartment, just in case. The best part was that Josh looked at "Aunt Jeannie" as a very cool companion rather than a babysitter and was happy to have her come and stay.

Amy felt lucky that at fifteen, Josh was still much more into video games than girls. She knew his friends would come and hang out after school, and Jeannie would easily handle any extra mouths to feed. Amy had gone shopping the night before to make sure the house was fully stocked. Now she just needed to get the last details sorted out at the office and she would be ready to go!

She dropped her soda can into the recycle bin and headed out the door. She'd be on her way in less than 24 hours.

Chapter 4. Carol

This was not how she wanted to spend her last hour at the office.

"I'm sure it will all work out fine." Carol smiled and ushered the young woman out her door. Whew. Hopefully that would be the last crisis for the day!

She turned back to her desk and reopened the e-mail with her list of "to do's" and the status of various projects for Eileen, her second-in-command. Once she had the list close to final, she'd get Eileen in to review it with her, then send her "out of office" e-mail and be on her way! Her bag sat in the corner, a reminder to finish and get to the airport. The flight was not until 5:30 p.m., but her little sister Amy was scheduled to arrive at 3:00 p.m. They wanted to catch up before they saw everyone else, but they also wanted to sleep as much as possible on the flight so they would be fresh when they arrived in Paris.

Carol reviewed her list. The Board meeting was not for three weeks, which gave her time to finalize that agenda after she got back. Eileen was tracking the various solicitation letters they'd sent out for grants for next year. Non-profits were definitely having to reach further this year for funding, and though Carol could see that most of their donors were still giving, they were, in general, giving less. The shortfall was sizeable enough that it could lead to layoffs.

Carol had been too busy to dwell on it, but she missed her sisters and could use their company in these stressful times. She knew she wouldn't agree with all of the advice they'd hand out, but she also knew that they would *always* have her best interests at heart. She frankly couldn't say that about anyone else in her life now.

Carol had bought food for the long weekend and had written out both kids' schedules for George, since logistics was yet another of the many jobs he left for her to manage, and teenage schedules could be challenging. Gwen, a junior in high school, was on the volleyball team and would expect a parent spectator at her game. Carol wasn't sure George even knew where the gym was. Brian, a freshman, would have his last track meet on Saturday and would need a ride. He wouldn't care who drove him, but George would either have to arrange it or do it himself. It was amazing to her how "busy" George always was, yet he never seemed to do anything productive. It was up to her to keep their daily life moving forward, so it would be interesting to see how he handled her absence. There was only so much preparation even she could do. She would be in Paris. George should be perfectly capable of getting through five days without her. At least she hoped so.

Looking over the e-mail one last time, she printed it and buzzed Eileen's office. "Hey, I think I'm ready. Are you at a point where you could come sit with me for a couple of minutes?"

Eileen laughed. "I've been waiting for your call for the last half hour. You need to get out of here! I'll be right there."

Eileen arrived and sat down in front of Carol's desk. "I am *so* jealous. Paris for five days! And in an apartment! Where is it, again?" Eileen was now sixty-five and a grandmother of two. Her husband had passed away the year before, and with her daughter and grandchildren living in California, she had become more dependent on her colleagues for friendship. She also freely admitted that she was not a confident traveler and lived vicariously through the travel of others.

Carol looked sheepish. "I've been so busy trying to make sure you have everything you need I actually haven't even focused on that yet. I figured I'd look at Margot's description and my map after I got to the airport."

"You are unbelievable! Okay, give me your list and let's walk through everything quickly so you can be on your way. We will be fine. It's only five days, and two of those are a weekend—plus you said Margot has a laptop and Internet access."

"I know. It just feels like there are lots of loose ends right now."

"There are always lots of loose ends in this job! So what else is new?" Regretting her remark, Eileen switched to a more soothing tone. "Yes, this year is tighter financially, but you know we're always one step away from crisis—that's the life of a non-profit. Anyway, we've already gotten some good feedback on a couple of our letters. I'm confident that more money will come through before the Board meeting and you'll have something positive to report. Besides, you always set up contingency plans just in case. You always make us all look good!"

Carol sighed. "You're right. Worrying won't change anything."

Eileen looked down at the list. "It looks like I have the contacts for the various pending grants. Any personnel issues I should know about? I saw Julie leaving and she looked like she'd been crying."

"Personal problems. You know these young people: every bump in a relationship is a major crisis. Apparently she is feeling like she and Jeff aren't communicating right now. I just asked, 'What are your plans for the weekend?' and I got a full litany about how they don't understand each other, what should she do, etc."

Eileen laughed and nodded. "Why don't you try not listening? Then people wouldn't dump their worries on you."

"Good advice, but hard for me to follow!"

"I know. Right now you've got a trip to take and you need to forget about Julie's troubles."

Carol sighed. "You're right. I have enough on my mind with the Board meeting, the funders, the big gala in six months...."

"Stop, stop!" Eileen put up her hand. "Anything else that I really need to be aware of in the next few days?"

"Just check in with Pat on the attendance for the meeting. And if we don't have a fifty percent response by the end of the day on Monday, I would like another reminder email to go out to the Board members."

"That's easy." Eileen smiled. "You have to promise you'll totally enjoy yourself and tell me all about it when you get back. And take pictures!"

Carol nodded and stood up to give her a hug. "Thanks for being such a great friend and great 'second-in-command.' I want you to know I do feel totally confident that you will keep everything completely under control in my absence."

"No you don't," Eileen answered cheerfully. "You wouldn't be you if you didn't worry about it. Now, get out of here. Send me an e-mail when you get there. I want to know when you're starting your wonderful adventure."

"I promise." Carol hesitated for just a moment, then clicked "send" on her "out of the office" e-mail. She picked up her bag and grinned suddenly. "Why do I feel like I'm playing hooky?"

"Because you are. Get out of here!" Eileen gave her a gentle push.

"I'm on my way," Carol thought, punching the elevator button. "At least, as long as I don't get stuck in the elevator."

Good grief! She couldn't even get out of the building without creating something to worry about. Enough. She was off on her adventure, and she could not *wait* to reconnect with her sisters in a fun, faraway place.

Chapter 5. Margot

I woke up just as the flight attendants started serving breakfast. I felt like I'd gotten enough sleep, eyes not too gritty. Did I look decent enough to face everyone? I got up and went into the lavatory to take a look at myself and brush my teeth. Well, not too bad. Hair a little flat, but mascara not too smeared. Scrutinizing myself in the mirror, I felt pretty good. Not too many wrinkles yet around my eyes or mouth. I had made the switch this year to full "color" from "highlights" and my hair was back to being a mid-shade of brown. My hairstyles had gotten shorter as the years went by and I had also finally gotten rid of that last ten pounds that had hung on since the boys were born. It had taken seventeen years, but it had finally happened.

Returning to my seat, I closed my eyes and tried to remember how Sophie and Carol had looked the last time I had seen them. Would we feel awkward and self-conscious, or would it be just like old times? Since Amy had seen everyone over these last few months, she could help with any strained conversations as we all got to know each other again.

I hoped all the flights had gone as planned. I had told them we would find each other in baggage claim. The old terminal at De Gaulle was confusing, with the baggage carousels wrapped around an open atrium, but we'd eventually find each other. As always, I was anxious to get to the apartment and feel I was "home," but I knew the excitement of sharing the apartment with my sisters would override my impatience.

As it turned out, I found a coffee stand just past the passport and customs area and realized it was the perfect spot to wait for everyone. I bought my *café crème* and a croissant with joy—Parisian food again!—then pulled out my book to wait, glancing up each time the area filled with the latest arrivals.

I looked up and saw Amy before she saw me. For a split second I saw her from a stranger's perspective. She was gorgeous, with her wild hair and huge blue eyes with eye shadow to match. She was wearing a bright flowered top over dark blue leggings. So much for my suggestion to "not look too American." At forty-seven, she still had a youthful energy that matched her bright colors. She was "full bodied," as American as you were likely to see, and not at all ashamed of it. She walked with confidence, more self-confidence than I'd seen in her during my last visit to see Mom.

Right behind Amy came Carol, who paused a little to one side of the crowd flowing through the passport check station. No change there. She was the observer and worrier of the family, the one who took time to review all new situations before deciding on her course of action. She was blending into the background and letting Amy get all the attention, as usual. It gave her time to figure out what was going on around her and how she wanted to fit in. Carol looked a little tired and slightly nervous. She was conservatively dressed in tan slacks and a brown-and-white top. She was not as tall as Amy, and her blond hair, cut short and curling around her face, was streaked with gray.

I stood up from my lookout spot. Both saw me at almost the same time and Amy broke into a run and grabbed me in a huge hug.

"Girlfriend, you look *fantastic!* How can that be, when I know you just got off a seven-hour flight like we did?" She grinned at me, her eyes sparkling.

I hugged her tightly. "You look great too! Both of you!" I turned her loose to hug Carol, who gave me a quick kiss on the cheek as well. "I am *so* glad you guys are here! How were the flights?"

Amy sighed. "Long, baby, long. I'm so glad Carol was on the second one so we could get some chatting in before we slept. Or tried to! Right, Carol?"

"I didn't sleep much, but that's because I was so excited about getting here. I still can't believe we're in France! And that I don't have to solve anyone's problems for five whole days." She paused and looked at me in mock worry. "You don't expect me to solve your problems, do you? Or make any decisions at all? Because we're depending on you to do all of that."

I laughed and shook my head. "With all the talking we're going to do for the next five days, I'm sure we will solve something. Maybe just world peace; who knows? Okay, see that luggage area over there? That is where your bags are coming in. I'll order for you while you get your luggage. We have about an hour till Sophie arrives. What can I buy you ladies?"

Amy groaned. "Please tell me they have Diet Coke and not just coffee?"

"Of course they do. But you have to call it by its French name, *Coca Light*."

"Call it what you want, I just want to drink one. Oh, and maybe eat something. What's our plan for eating?"

"If you're hungry, let's order you something here. After we get Sophie, it'll be a good hour before we get to the apartment. Once there, though, we can have a true French breakfast of fresh baguettes and butter. Or, depending on what time it is, we can go down to the café and get lunch. Plus I asked my friend, Monique, to do some shopping for us, so there should be food at the apartment when we arrive."

Amy opted for a croissant and a *Coca Light*, and I encouraged Carole to have her first genuine *café crème*. They left, but soon returned, each with her "one bag." They settled around a small table while I was ordering.

After I returned with their food, Amy spoke. "Listening to you speak makes me think we'll be fine on the French front! Is this the coolest thing ever? I can't believe you actually bought a place over here. I guess since you're on the East Coast it's pretty easy to come over, right?"

"Definitely. Literally seven hours and I'm here. I have friends who drive the same amount of time to get to a beach house in North Carolina."

Amy laughed. "I guess that's true, but it takes a different attitude to buy a second home in Paris than one in North Carolina!"

"True," I grinned. "Just wait! You'll love Paris as much as I do!

Amy took another bite of her croissant and exclaimed, "I'm liking this already!"

Carol said, "In our area, the other thing people do is buy a house on one of the lakes. George and I have thought about that ourselves, but it hasn't worked out so far."

"You mean that consultant husband of yours hasn't landed the big monster contract yet?" Amy teased. "He does understand that he can't depend on you to make the big bucks if you keep doing this non-profit thing, right?"

Carol smiled. "He does know that. Somehow it just hasn't come together yet." She seemed a little uncomfortable and changed the subject. "Margot, talk to us about where the apartment is. I looked on my map but that doesn't really mean anything to me."

"It's in the 11th *arrondisement*. Paris is divided into neighborhoods called *arrondisements* that spiral out from the center." I grabbed a salt shaker and said, "Imagine this is Notre Dame. It sits on a small island in the middle of the Seine, the river that divides Paris into the Left Bank and Right Bank." I took two spoons and laid them down on each side of the salt shaker. "This lower side is the Left Bank. That is where the Latin Quarter is, with lots of students and tourists. That was the only area I really knew from my time here as a student, but Paul and I knew we didn't want to live in that area because it's too noisy. Keep in mind that most of Paris does not have air-conditioning, so if you live in an apartment, you will have the windows open a lot. Loud singing at 2:00 a.m. is not my idea of a peaceful home life." Amy and Carol both nodded in agreement. "So we opened our search to other parts of the city, keeping in mind that we wanted to be within easy walking distance of the center, but not too expensive. A friend of mine suggested the 10th and 11th *arrondisements* on the Right Bank, because they're considered 'up and coming' while still affordable." I placed some sugar packets on the imaginary Right Bank to represent my neighborhood. "So here is where we ended up, in the 11th. It's an area that continues to get more interesting—it's cheap, so it's where new chefs start restaurants and entrepreneurs open fun boutiques."

"You mean it's not cooler just because you live there?" Amy asked with open-eyed innocence. "Ouch!" she added, as I punched her arm in response.

"No, smartass, but it definitely makes us look brilliant for buying there. We're about a twenty-minute walk from Notre Dame and right above the Marais, which is the old Jewish quarter. It's one of the few areas that has places open on Sunday."

"Sounds great," Carol said. "I'm looking forward to lots of walking around."

"We will be doing lots of walking, for sure! It's a great city for that. Every street has great architecture, wonderful little courtyards, and fun little shops that you'll stumble across and then wonder how they ever survive."

"So are you happy you bought here?" Carol asked.

"I am *so* happy. And Paul is too, or at least he says he is. He hasn't been here nearly as much as I have because of his work, but we talk a lot about all the time we'll spend here and the things we'll do when the kids are on their own."

Carol smiled. "That's great to hear. Maybe George and I will figure out our own version of a getaway someday." I noticed her eyes did not seem to mirror her smile and vowed to get to the bottom of that before our time here was through. Carol was one of the most giving people I knew, and I fervently hoped that she was happy.

Looking at my watch I said, "Sophie should be popping out any time now." We all watched the entrance expectantly.

"There she is!" Amy squealed and jumped up, then ran to give Sophie a hug. Same light brown hair, now with highlights. She had cut it so that it came just below her ears and framed her face. Same brown eyes, already twinkling as she saw Amy flying towards her. But one change for sure: she was definitely thinner in her dark slacks and green sweater. Amy swung her around and whispered something in her ear that had them both laughing loudly. No such thing as staying in the background with those two. Several people around them were staring, some with smiles and some with the disdainful look that Parisians seem able to pull off better than anyone. Both women came back to the table. I got up to give Sophie a hug and then stepped back to look her up and down. "You are looking *so* good!" I could not stop beaming at her. "This busy life of bossing lots of people around seems to agree with you."

She smiled back. "Well thanks, Sis. You don't look half bad yourself." We all four kept looking at each other and I knew I had the same silly grin on my face that they had on theirs. For being 53, 52, 50 and 47, we all looked pretty darn good. "Okay, let's admit it right here—this was a *killer* idea to get together," I finally said. "Whose idea was it? Oh, mine, that's right."

"I hate to give you a big head, but you're right; this is going to be great!" Amy agreed. "Okay, Sophie, do you want coffee before we go, or should we all just get moving?"

"Whoa, whoa, let's get her suitcase first!" Carol had always been the balance to Amy's impulsiveness.

"Good idea," said Sophie. "I can wait for coffee until we get to the apartment."

"Shall we splurge on a taxi?" I asked.

"No question!" Amy piped up. "Lead the way!" She gulped the last of her *Coca Light*, swept my impromptu map of Paris off the table, and stuffed the various cups and paper into a trash container nearby.

I had been to Paris countless times since my college days, but with all my sisters here everything seemed different. In a few moments I would be sharing with them a very important part of my life. There wasn't any reason for me to be nervous... was there?

Chapter 6. Margot

"We're here!" I announced, as the taxi pulled up in front of a large brown door.

"Cool," breathed Amy. "The door is so *tall*."

"I know. The building was built in 1890. Once upon a time this door had to accommodate horses and carriages."

Amy looked confused. "What do you mean? Horses and carriages went in the door?"

"Yep. You'll see when we get inside. This door leads into a courtyard. The apartment is actually in the back."

I gave Sophie some euros for the taxi driver, who was unloading our bags, then I went up and punched the access code and pushed the heavy door open. "I'll give you all the codes in case we go out separately. There's a code for this door, and also for the door to our building, which you enter from the courtyard."

"I don't want to speak for you guys, but I'm going wherever Margot goes," Amy said with a smile. "I won't need to remember any codes."

"Me neither," Sophie and Carol both said simultaneously, then burst out laughing. "We always used to do that, remember?" Sophie added. Carol nodded and squeezed Sophie's arm.

We seized the handles of our luggage and started across the courtyard.

"Yikes, that's a lot of noise." Carol looked around quickly to see if anyone might be irritated by the sound of the luggage rolling across the cobblestones.

"Don't worry. People are used to that kind of noise from the courtyard. See this door to the right? That's where the *guardienne* lives. That's the same sound we hear every time she rolls the trash cans out to the street.

She also delivers the mail and does general cleaning. If you ask, she will come and clean your apartment for an additional charge, but I can tell you it's not her strong suit. You'll probably meet her at some point while you're here. She's very nice but doesn't speak English, so just smile and say *'Bonjour, Madame.'*"

"*Bonjour, Madame,*" they all chorused.

I couldn't help grinning. The camaraderie was already coming back and it felt nice to be together again.

We reached the second door and I punched in the code and pulled it open. There was a tiny entryway that had a door on each side leading to apartments and a small elevator in the center. It smelled slightly musty and the wall across from the elevator was in need of a coat of paint. "The elevator is typical European: tiny. I would suggest that one person ride up with everyone's luggage and the rest of us walk. It's just two flights up."

Sophie immediately volunteered and I held the outer glass door for her as she pushed the luggage in, and then warned her not to get caught by the second, inner gate that had to close completely before the elevator could function. The rest of us trooped up the two flights.

"As you can see, there are just two doors on each landing. We are the left door. Everyone got it?"

The elevator arrived and the small landing was suddenly packed with women and luggage. I squeezed my way over to the door and unlocked it. "Welcome to my 'home away from home.' It's not big, but it's all mine."

Amy was first through the door. Light was streaming in on the right from the living room and Monique had put fresh flowers on the small dining table in the corner. Amy breathed out slowly. "Wow, this is way cool. Look at this ceiling. It has to be ten feet tall!"

"Pretty close. When we were looking at apartments, we were told that there are three architectural features to look for if you want a building from the late 19th century: high ceilings with crown molding, a herringbone pattern in the hardwood floors, and a marble fireplace with a framed mirror above it. As you can see, we have all three!"

Sophie said, "Margot, it's really gorgeous. And you have decorated it so well. It's simple, warm and inviting."

"Thank you! That's what we were trying for. We obviously started with nothing, so it was a chance to have some fun furnishing it with whatever we wanted. Well, within reason, anyway! Also we made our choices based on this apartment being our second home, not a place we would be renting out."

Carol pointed to a doorway on the far side of the living room. "Where does that go?"

"That's the second bedroom. It's small, but efficient. There is a trundle bed that we'll pull out from under the twin bed, and once they're both up, that's about all you can fit! After our Rock, Paper, Scissors exercise in the taxi, that's where Amy and

Sophie will be sleeping." I turned back toward the hallway where we had entered.

"Let me give you the rest of the grand tour." I laughed and pointed across the hall. "That door leads to the master bedroom. Its window looks out over the courtyard, while the small bedroom and living room windows look out over the small street at the back of the building."

Sophie moved across the hall and opened the door, then opened her mouth in a mock look of astonishment. "And who chose this color?"

"I know! Who would think orange would be a good color for a bedroom? Actually, the previous owners painted it this color, but we liked it so much we left it. You'll see they also modernized the kitchen and bathroom, bless their hearts."

Sophie looked around slowly. "You know, it does work. And the artwork is perfect." The others murmured in agreement.

"I pick up little paintings from *artistes* around the city. Maybe you'll find something you like!"

I felt a sense of relief and realized suddenly how much I'd worried about this moment, knowing how important their opinions were to me. I felt a weight lifting from my shoulders.

"On to the rest of the tour. You can see straight ahead of you is the toilet, or W.C., as they call it here. Literally, that's all that's in there—a toilet. And the door to the right of that is the bathroom, which is to say the sink, and a bathtub with a showerhead. It's nice, especially in a small place like this, to have the toilet in a separate room. The washer and dryer are in the bathroom, stacked on top of each other. And believe me, they are *not* American size! If you have undies or something like that to wash, we can do it, but don't give me big heavy stuff. Not only would it take forever to wash, but also forever to dry. The dryer is not connected to a vent outside, so it basically just heats up the place."

Amy laughed. "Wow! Glad we're here in May and don't need big sweatshirts."

"Exactly. And in five days I figure we can't get too dirty. Last stop is just down this little hall to the kitchen. Again, small, but very efficient."

Carol looked around for moment then asked, "Okay, you've got me. Where is the fridge?"

I laughed. "Right here behind this panel. The fridge is the top half and the freezer is the bottom half. From the outside it looks like the rest of the cabinets." I opened the refrigerator and saw that Monique, as promised, had bought butter, milk and juice.

Amy peered over my shoulder. "Not much space in there, girlfriend. Thank goodness we didn't bring our big growing boys here. We'd never be able to stock enough food!"

"The lifestyle here is to shop for fresh food every day or two. There is an open-air market just a block away on Tuesdays and Saturdays that you guys will love. We can get our veggies and fruit there tomorrow, and get our meat from the butcher shop nearby. There is cheese at the market, and also in a cute little *fromagerie* near the butcher, as well as a small grocery for milk and napkins and those kinds of things."

Sophie smiled. "Sounds like you've got everything at your doorstep."

"We really do. The hardest part is remembering that you have to carry home whatever you buy! We'll take my little bag with wheels on it when we do our first run for *Coca Light* and wine. Those bottles get very heavy."

Amy laughed. "Glad to hear that you're keeping my best interests in mind. So what should we do next?"

"Let's see. It's 11:30 Paris time. How about we take showers and get that airplane grime off, then head down to the café for lunch?"

Amy nodded her head vigorously. "Is there enough hot water for four of us?"

"Amazingly, yes, if you don't stay in there for too long. The water heater is small but it gets the job done!"

"I'll be quick, I promise!" said Amy. "May I go first?" Everyone nodded. "Let me just grab my shampoo from my bag."

"There's shampoo in there, but use yours if you'd prefer."

Amy returned, bulging cosmetics bag in hand, and I got a towel for her from above the washer/dryer. "Oh, I didn't tell you about one of the other fun features." I took her towel and draped it over the rack. "The rack is heated so your towel will be nice and toasty for you when you get out."

"Man you know how to live right! I don't think I'm going back home."

Amy closed the door and I headed back to the kitchen where Carol and Sophie were opening various cabinets and commenting on what they found. The espresso machine led to interest in lattes all around and I shooed them out as I heated the milk.

It felt funny to be telling my two older sisters what to do. Now, that was a change from the past! What else would change in our relationships on this trip? I could hear them talking quietly and tried to remember how long it had been since they'd seen each other. I also wondered what they were talking about. Impressions of the trip so far? Impressions of me? They had no idea how much I needed this trip right now, and about the stresses I was facing at home. I knew I was close to a breaking point and that I needed someone to talk to besides Paul. There were things going on that felt too delicate to trust to friends, even close ones. Could my sisters help? Would they want to help? I sent up a silent prayer as I headed back to the living room.

Chapter 7. Amy

Standing in the hot shower, Amy let the tiredness from the trip slide off her with the water. She could tell already that this had been the right decision. It had been fun to watch the reactions as her sisters saw each other again for the first time. She knew Margot had been surprised at Sophie's weight loss and wondered what conversations would come from that. Body weight and shape had always been a sensitive topic at home, but they might be able to discuss it now that everyone was older and more comfortable with their respective sizes. They were definitely already falling into the easy banter that they'd shared as kids.

She had texted Josh when she landed to let him know she'd arrived, knowing that he would respond when he woke up. So let's see, what time was it at home? It was about noon here in Paris, which meant it was six in the morning on the East Coast, and that meant it was three in the morning in

Las Vegas. The next question for Amy's befuddled brain was: what day is it? She'd caught her first flight at 10:00 Thursday morning and flown Thursday night, so this must be Friday. So she should hear from Josh in about four hours as he got ready for school. That would be four in the afternoon here.

She let her mind drift briefly back to work and her concerns about Andrew. She would talk to her sisters about him and see what they thought. Maybe she was being paranoid, but she didn't think so.

Thinking about work led, as it always did, to thinking about money, and that was always a tough topic. She and Melinda were still taking minimal salaries so they could pay the staff and the office rent. She was working on getting big contracts with two large hotels, but she was having trouble getting final signatures on the agreements. There always seemed to be one more question from corporate or one more person who had to weigh in on the decision. "Maybe that's a question for these fine businesswomen this weekend," she thought. They might very well be able to offer advice on how to close the deals.

Amy had come a long way from being the wild child she had been in her youth, but she was realizing that her "leap first" attitude, which had given her the courage to start her own business, also meant that she didn't always think things through as thoroughly as she should. She had avoided making any huge mistakes as an entrepreneur so far, although Andrew might be her first. Why did she always have to "live and learn?" If she was being honest with herself, she knew that what she really needed was broader financial advice, and it would be very hard to ask her sisters for that. They were all so successful, and she was still having trouble making ends meet. Here were three impartial people to consult, but that had to be weighed against the danger they would use information about her perilous financial situation to judge her. Her sensitivity about this issue had been building over many years, and now it was a mountain of insecurity that she wasn't sure she could overcome.

Everything for them seemed so perfect—not only financially, but also in their marriages—and here she was, 47, divorced, and still having trouble paying the mortgage. Where had she failed? Why was she not able to get a break in this world? Could she really be that incompetent? Was she missing something? Did they all have the perfect recipe for success and they somehow forget to tell her about it? "No," she told herself. "You know you are a competent, smart woman who has had a couple of tough breaks. Your chance will come. Admit it, you always somehow choose the wrong road to get anywhere."

After high school, frustrated with education and the "system," she had worked for a couple of years before realizing how important a college degree was for advancement anywhere. After she earned her degree, she spent a couple of years trying to decide what she wanted to do, and then went to work for a great guy who had taught her a lot, but who didn't know how to manage people. Eventually he ran his business into the ground. And along the way she'd married another great guy who, as it turned out, also had no business sense. Man, she could certainly pick them!

On the positive side, she now owned her own business and it was growing, albeit slowly. Melinda was a great partner and friend. Josh was a good kid—at least, most of the time. She would just have to keep thinking about things and figure them out on her own. That was how she'd managed so far.

Well, there were three others waiting to take their turn in the shower. She turned the water off and reached for her towel, which, as Margot had promised, was toasty warm. She wrapped herself up in it, wrapped a smaller towel around her head, and opened the door, letting out a puff of steam into the hallway. "Margot, I *want* one of these heater things. This warm towel is heating me up all over, if you know what I mean! Who's next?"

Sophie called out from the living room. "Carol is next. And don't start talking like that. You know how Margot gets all embarrassed."

"Oh excuuuussse meeeeee…. She is a grown woman, for heaven's sake!"

Margot laughed. "It's okay, Sophie. I think I can handle it—just barely. Get it? Carol, get your buns in there. Amy, I put the blow dryer on the counter so you can start your beautification while Carol showers."

"Fine, I can see who thinks she's in charge of everyone! Carol, come on in."

As she combed her hair, Amy tried to push the frustration with her financial situation to the back of her mind. She would be hearing about Andrew any moment, and she hoped she could come up with solutions, or at least possible steps towards future solutions, over the next few days. She did not want her worries to feel like a dark cloud hanging over everything. But how could she ever get the courage to share her problems with everyone? How could she confess to someone like Margot, who owned an apartment in Paris, for God's sake—that she was still making a mess of her life?

Chapter 8. Sophie

With Amy and Carol in the bathroom, and Margot puttering around in the kitchen, singing softly under her breath, Sophie had the living room to herself. She was reclining in what she decided was the most comfortable leather chair ever made. Margot had showed her how to tilt it back and bring up the footrest. She was content just sipping her latte and looking around. It really was a terrific room, full of light, with its high ceilings and tall windows. The paintings on the wall reflected Margot's love for bright primary colors, and the furniture was all soft browns and muted reds. She looked up at the pale pink and white chandelier, which looked like alabaster. Its soft light added to the comfortable, calm feeling of the room. Leaning back, she allowed herself to truly relax, and realized it had been a long time since she had done so.

If asked, Sophie would not have said she was tense in her daily life, but being around her sisters again made her realize that in Salt Lake she always kept herself slightly distant and watchful, careful not to make any mistakes that could be held against her. It was understandable at work. She was at an important point in her career, and she sometimes felt the slope was more slippery than it appeared and her position more tenuous. Being a woman was both an advantage and a disadvantage. Sometimes she could speak up and say things that men could not or would not. Her colleagues knew her remarks were meant as constructive criticism, not competition. On the other hand, she still felt that in the accounting business there were always men, both above her and at her level, who were sure they could do her job better. Some were threatened by her quiet confidence, acquired after twenty years in the business. Physical appearance was also important, and she sometimes worried that not being the "perfect" 36-24-36 was a disadvantage. There were days when other factors piled on top of one another and she felt like she was back in high school.

Now, home was another issue. Why would she be tense there? She had two wonderful boys, a wonderful husband, and lived in a wonderful house. She made a great salary, and Roger seemed happy in his roles as househusband and head of the booster club at school. When they were first married, he had been a teacher at the local high school, but as her job responsibilities grew and she repeatedly was asked to relocate, it became difficult for Roger to find work in new school systems every couple of years. Often the only available position was as a substitute teacher. He found that role more frustrating than fulfilling—switching classrooms daily, never staying long enough in any school system to become friends with other teachers, or to see if he was making a difference with the kids. Eventually he quit altogether.

Roger was thinking about training for a new type of job when Sophie got pregnant with Bobby. After her maternity leave, it made no sense to pay for daycare with Roger out of work. By the time Jeremy came along, Sophie was in yet another new job, this time in Chicago, and so once again she went back to work and Roger took care of both boys. He was a wonderful father, always playing with the kids, reading to them, taking them to the park and museums, and using his teaching skills to enhance their learning.

As the boys moved into middle school and then high school, Roger became very involved with the booster club, working at the concession stands during games and attending most practices. In his youth, Roger had been a standout soccer player and it was obvious he loved being part of a team's daily rituals. His physical condition had always been important to him and he enjoyed running during the practices. He still played soccer recreationally.

Having Roger as such an active father made it easier for Sophie to spend the time she felt she needed to at the office and at work-related evening events. She felt guilty sometimes about the games she'd missed, or the awards ceremonies she'd been late for, but she knew the boys were well taken care of. She also knew that the money she brought in made their lives comfortable and secure. It didn't seem as if their lifestyle could be making her feel ill at ease. By now she should be reconciled to their roles. There were times when she worried about Roger, and about the time they were no longer spending together, but consoled herself with the fact that they would make up for it after the boys left for college.

Roger had been angry with her when she had first brought up this trip. He was unhappy with the decision to travel such a long distance because it added to the total time away. The location had been a group decision, not hers alone, so she could justify it from that standpoint, but still, it was a trip for pleasure rather than for business. The truth was that he never got to go anywhere. Maybe that was part of his frustration? He'd been very angry when she had made it clear that she felt she should, and would, go. It was the first actual argument they'd had in a long time, and it had scared her. She realized now that her fear stemmed not from the argument itself, but from the fact that they had not argued in a long time. Why was that? Was that because they got along so well? Or was it because their lives had drifted so far apart that they had little reason to argue?

"Sophie! Your turn!" Carol appeared around the corner, her hair wrapped and her face shining. "It's a great shower!"

Sophie pushed her thoughts aside. "Great! I'll be right there—as soon as I can figure out how to get out of this chair!" She found the lever, dropped off her cup in the kitchen, and headed for the bathroom. Amy was just putting the finishing touches on her face. Before Amy noticed her, Sophie had a chance to watch her unobserved. "She really is a beautiful woman," Sophie thought. "I wonder what's going on in her life right now? There was never a chance to really talk when I was in town for Mom."

Amy drawled. "I'm about as beautiful as I can get—at least with these particular products. Maybe what I need is some makeup from Paris!"

"You are beautiful indeed, little sister. Maybe you can give me some helpful hints while we're here?"

"I should say so! It's definitely time for you to stop being a minimalist on the makeup front! We girls of a certain age benefit greatly from enhancement, whether structural or cosmetic."

Sophie laughed. "You always had a way with words! Okay, I'll call you when I'm out and you can give me some pointers."

"Glad to. This is basically a long slumber party, right?" Grinning, Amy headed out to the living room. "Carol, where are you? What makeup do you use? Sophie needs help and I need to see what we have so we can set up a makeover session later." Amy's voice muted as Sophie closed the door and turned on the shower. Did she really look that terrible? Would it make any difference if she showed up at work wearing more makeup? Wasn't she employed for her expertise? But losing weight had made a difference—maybe not to the other people at work, but to her. She knew she felt more confident now that she looked less... matronly. Why hadn't her sisters said anything about it?

Sophie felt an unfamiliar jolt of rebelliousness. Well, she hadn't lost weight to please her sisters; she'd done it for herself. Next she was going to invest in some makeup. She would return from this vacation a changed woman.

Chapter 9. Margot

I hopped in the shower after Sophie and, when I came out of the bathroom, I was greeted by the sound of laughter coming from the living room.

"What's going on out here?"

Amy smiled at me as I came around the corner. "We were just comparing makeup notes. Or should I say, comparing hypothetical makeup notes, because some of us don't seem to know anything, or use anything."

Sophie said with a hint of defiance, "I just never thought I needed anything."

"Yeah, right." Amy's look of disgust was comical. "Let me just tell you. I work with a couple of sweet young things who are about twenty-five. I've seen them with and without makeup and, even at that age, they are much cuter *with* than *without*. Youth only goes so far—and it doesn't last long!"

"And of course, as you get older," Carol interjected, "you need to cover stuff up as well as emphasize the good stuff."

Amy nodded. "Sophie, you have nice eyes but they're a little small, so you need to put on some eyeliner and mascara to bring them out."

Sophie turned to me and I nodded. "I've had a few makeup sessions at department stores, and it has become obvious to me that I need the same approach. My eyes are small, too." Sophie looked a little dejected, so I added, "And my lashes are too light, so unless I use mascara, you can't see them at all."

"We'll start small and work our way up," said Amy. "I'll do your eyes, then we'll all go to lunch."

Fifteen minutes later we were on our way. Sophie was pleased with her fresh new look, and everyone agreed that Amy did good work. I scooted everyone out of the apartment and turned to lock the door.

"Wow that's a cool key," said Amy. "I didn't notice it before."

"When you think about it, the design is over a hundred years old. I think this door is original."

"I need to keep reminding myself of how old things are over here," said Amy. "It makes you take extra care of everything, I'm sure!"

"You know it! We don't rent the place out very often, but when we do I'm very careful to get the key back immediately."

We started down the winding stairs. Amy looked back up at me. "I thought you said you didn't use this place as a rental."

"We only rent to people we know directly and trust. Think about it this way. If you broke anything, even just a wine glass for instance, you'd feel bad about it. If I rented the apartment to someone who didn't know me, and they broke something, it wouldn't mean as much to them because to them this place is 'just' a rental."

Amy nodded. "Makes sense. Okay, so I can rent it from you, but my friends can't?" She smiled.

"Right. You just tell me when and you can have it—for $150 a night, of course."

"Is that with the family discount?"

"Nope. The only ones with a discount are Mom and Dad, and Paul's parents. Actually they stay for free, so they get a 100% discount, I guess. We decided early on that we can't juggle who gets what discount, so no one does."

"I know how much Mom and Dad have loved coming here. Do Paul's parents like using the apartment too?"

"His mom does. His grandmother lived in France for about ten years, so he and his family visited often. His mother is very comfortable traveling here."

"That's great. It's nice to think that other family members enjoy it too."

We exited out to the courtyard and walked back across the cobblestones.

"Good thing I brought flats," Amy remarked. "I'd hate to break an ankle on Day One."

"Here's the button you have to push to get out of the courtyard door," I said. Pushing open the heavy door, I continued, "Out and turn left."

We walked up one block and there, set back from the street with small tables out front, was a small café.

"This is where Paul and I like to come for a quick lunch."

"My stomach is definitely ready," said Amy. "Anyone else?"

"Absolutely!" Sophie agreed. "Carol?"

"I have to admit I am now officially starving!"

I smiled. "Let's eat inside. It's a little chilly, and besides, the smokers sit out here." Once inside and settled, I looked around. "They've renovated since I was last here and created an interior area for smokers. See how they can shut that door to close off that area? Smart move on their part."

Carol spoke up. "I read about the new no-smoking law. It must have been horrible before with such a small amount of space between tables."

I nodded. "There were times we'd have someone smoking a foot away while we were still eating. You can't taste anything when your face is full of smoke! Now that's gone, unless you're sitting outside."

The waiter passed out menus. "Another nice thing about this place is that it lists the items in English underneath the French name. I won't guarantee that the English is always accurate or understandable, but it's a start."

There was silence for a few moments, then Carol asked, "Do you have any suggestions?"

"I tend to get either an omelet, which comes with salad or *frites*, or I get one of the large salads. See, this one has goat cheese on little pieces of toast, and country ham, and walnuts. It's very good. Salads always come dressed with French vinaigrette, just so you know. Another good thing is a *Croque Monsieur*, basically an open faced ham and cheese sandwich, but—being French—it has a divine sauce on it."

After some discussion, I motioned to the waiter and gave him all four orders. After he left, I looked at Sophie. "So, Sophie, are you ready to tell us your secret?"

Sophie looked confused and a little uncomfortable so I added, "I want to know what you're doing to have lost so much weight and to look so terrific!"

Her face cleared and she grinned broadly. "Thanks! It's been a slow process, but I finally realized that losing weight was not about crazy fad diets. It's about making good choices."

I nodded. "That's something I figured out, too. I hate to say it, but I guess I just don't need as much food as I used to, you know?"

"Exactly!" Sophie added, "And don't waste calories on things that aren't worth it." She paused. "The other thing, of course, is exercise, which is always tough to fit into a busy lifestyle."

Carol jumped in. "I try to do little things, like park at the far end of the parking lot at the mall so I have further to walk. Or park on the other side from the store that I plan to visit so I have to walk through the mall to get there."

Amy laughed. "For shopaholics like me, that could be dangerous! Who knows what I would find along the way?"

Everyone laughed. There was a pause and Amy added, "Seriously, Sophie, you really do look fantastic and I am *so* proud of you!"

I nodded and added, "The good news is that we are going to walk a *ton* over the next five days, so don't worry about the exercise piece of your new regimen."

"I'm looking forward to it! This will be the most enjoyable walking I've done in a long time. Believe me, Salt Lake doesn't lend itself to scenic walks. Lots of desert between boring buildings."

"None of that around here!" There was a short silence as the food arrived. "By the way, any of you can feel free to order your own food. I'm not trying to be the boss here."

"Understood," Amy drawled. "Unless they suddenly become fluent in English, I'm leaving that task to you. But not because I'm intimidated by a waiter. I'm afraid of ordering calf brains by mistake!"

I grinned. "Yes, that could happen. Guess I'll be your translator this trip."

Amy's smile turned mischievous. "Unless I find some handsome French dude to replace you."

"Believe me, there are several checking you out already. I'm not sure Paris is ready! You're the only single one among us, so I guess we'll all live vicariously through you!"

"I'll keep my eyes open." Amy's eyes twinkled.

Carol looked worried. "Amy, are you sure that would be a good idea?"

Amy laughed. "That's not even the question, my friend. Seriously, it's not something I'm even thinking about. But you know I can never resist a chance to freak out you conservative gals. Besides, I believe that we should always leave ourselves open to all possibilities."

Amy raised her glass in a toast. "To sisters, and to a great next five days. Let's hope that if we learn nothing else, we learn that we need not wait so long to get together again."

We all clinked our glasses together and drank.

"Hear, hear!"

It was nice to see Amy's mischievous streak resurface. That meant she was relaxing and having fun. But a part of me was wondering exactly what Amy meant by being open to "all possibilities." Had I opened a Pandora's box by mistake?

Chapter 10. Margot

Back at the apartment, everyone found a spot and got comfortable around the living room. Jet lag was starting to set in.

Sophie spoke first. "So, Margot, how much planning have you done for us already?"

"I came up with a few ideas, but really I want us to make the plans all together. It's worth making some sort of plan because otherwise four days will go by and we will be sitting around moaning that we haven't done anything."

"I agree," Sophie smiled. "Besides, as you know, I like being organized."

Amy laughed. "Who, you? Miss Bossy Pants? Nah...."

Sophie threw a pillow in her general direction, though her aim was not too precise.

"You know that has been your nickname since time began, so don't act like the shoe doesn't fit."

Sophie shrugged. "Ok, fine. But being able to take charge isn't all bad—I've made a decent living using that particular skill."

Amy backed off and turned to me. "Let's make sure we take advantage of this time together. Give us your ideas."

"Well, general ideas are the *Musée D'Orsay*, where a lot of the Impressionist paintings are—Amy, I know you like those; the *Grand Palais,* which has an exhibition on Marie Antoinette that could be fun; and the Cluny Museum, which has the tapestries of "The Lady and the Unicorn" that are very nice. We could add a walking tour of the Latin Quarter. We walk right past Notre Dame on our way, so we could stop there. Or we could go to the big flea market that's open on weekends. That's actually where this chandelier came from, by the way. Or we could go up to *Sacre Coeur*, a gorgeous cathedral at the highest point in Paris that has a great view of the city. There are street artists up there, and cheap places to buy French tablecloth material."

"Whoa, slow down, slow down!" Amy laughed. "Ladies?" She looked around the room. "Has anyone thought about what they want to do?"

Sophie spoke up first. "The Marie Antoinette exhibit sounds interesting."

Carol spoke up next. "I'd definitely like to walk around the Latin Quarter. Maybe see those tapestries if that fits with what else we're doing."

Amy nodded. "I want to see the Impressionist paintings. But we *are* going to do some shopping, too, aren't we? This sounds like too much culture for me!"

"*Bien sur!*" I grinned. "Of course!" I looked around at the reclining figures and at my watch. "It's already 2:30. I propose we take a short walk down into the Marais, the old Jewish district nearby, come back here for a nap, and then walk down to a nearby restaurant around 8:00 for dinner. How does that sound?" Everyone nodded.

"Tomorrow is Saturday, so that's one of the two days we can go to the open air market I was telling you about. We can wake up whenever we want, eat our Parisian breakfast of fresh bread and butter with coffee, and then a couple of us can go to the market and to the stores to buy snacks and stuff for dinner tomorrow night. I assume everyone's budget would appreciate some home cooking mixed in with some dining out?" Nods again all around. "In the afternoon, depending on the weather, we could go down to Notre Dame and then maybe walk along the streets of Ile St. Louis and window shop?"

Amy clapped her hands together with glee. "This is *so* cool! It all sounds fantastic!"

I grinned, sharing her excitement, though I'd done those walks many times. "I still feel that way, every time. There is always a new shop, or some new café, or some little park that I never noticed before." I paused. "It's a magical city."

Sophie looked skeptical. "There are lots of cool cities in the world. I, for one, am looking forward to exploring your 'magical' city, but with my eyes wide open, not full of stars."

"Fine, you can make your own judgments; but I'm telling you, it's a city that grows on you."

Carol jumped up. "Let's get moving, then, and burn off those amazing *frites* we had for lunch! What's the weather like out there?" Stepping up to the window, she looked out onto the street. "Some clouds, some blue sky, some gray spots." She looked back into the room. "It may be worth bringing an umbrella and a sweater, just in case."

"And so speaks the practical one in the bunch!" I went over and hugged her as I said it. "How have I managed without you to keep my feet on the ground?"

Everybody started getting up, stretching and looking for what they might like to bring. I felt sheepish as I said, "I just realized that I didn't mention this ahead of time, but my feeling is that "less is more" in terms of what you carry around with you. Does anyone have a small travel purse to wear across your chest? Either bring that or button everything into a front pocket. I have never had a problem, but there are definitely pickpockets—and in these tough economic times there will be more of them, I'm sure. Leave your passports here. Bring a driver's license, a credit card, and your debit card to get euros at the ATM around the corner. I'll bring a map and a bigger bag for bottled water and any treasures we find. I'll throw in a couple of those small, fold-up umbrellas, too. That should do it!"

"I'll put my stuff in my pocket, since I didn't know to bring a small travel purse— but that just means a shopping opportunity!" Amy grinned as she stuffed her license in her jeans.

For a moment the four of us looked at each other in amazement, not quite daring to believe we were really all together and in Paris. It occurred to me, as I looked around, that each succeeding daughter was less practical and more adventurous than the last. It was probably a good thing our parents stopped having kids when they did. Anyone after Amy would have been irrational and fearless!

Everybody grabbed their sweaters and, as I locked the door, the three of them locked arms and attempted to go down the narrow staircase together, bumping and scraping the walls on each side as they went. Amy's giggle was infectious and we were all out of breath by the time we got to the bottom. Maybe it was just the jet lag, but everyone was definitely feeling a little giddy. As we stepped onto the street, I said, "Are you ready, Paris? Here come the Mitchell Sisters!"

Chapter 11. Amy

Amy walked next to Carol, and behind Sophie and Margot. Every street was full of new and interesting things to look at—stores, people, clothes, and buildings.

"Man, I need to bring Josh back here," said Amy. "He would love all the people and the weird cars and, in particular, all the motorcycles."

She stopped at a shop window and gazed at the wonderful display of jewelry. Sophie and Margot came back to stand next to Amy and Carol. "Everything looks so beautiful!" Amy exclaimed.

Margot said, "I read somewhere that the presentation of anything and everything is very important to the French. See how creatively the necklaces are all stacked in varying patterns? It makes the display as interesting as the pieces within it."

Amy nodded. "You're right."

"By the way, that reminds me of a simple etiquette thing here. Salespeople take their jobs very seriously, so it is important to show your respect. When you enter a store, you should always greet the salesperson with a *'Bonjour Madame'* or *'Bonjour Monsieur.'* You will see a big difference in how you are treated in return, trust me."

Amy nodded. "I don't want to embarrass you, and I also don't want to be an 'ugly American', so I'll be on my best behavior."

Margot smiled. "You're definitely not an ugly anything!"

Amy smiled and, as they continued down the street, looked at her watch. Josh should be getting back to her soon. Her thoughts turned to home.

****

Amy was just finishing moving the mound of dishes and glasses from the sink to the dishwasher when the front door slammed and Josh came flying into the kitchen. He rounded the kitchen table and bent to give Amy a kiss on the cheek. "Hi, Mom!"

Amy smiled briefly before placing her hands on her hips. "What's the deal with all these dishes?"

Josh bowed his head. "Sorry, Mom. Jake and David were over and we were playing video games, then realized we were going to be late for basketball so...." His voice faded and he looked sheepish. "I thought I would get home before you."

"Josh, you need to make sure you give yourself time to clean up before you head out. I'm happy to have those guys come and hang out with you after school, but not if it makes the house a pigsty."

"I know, Mom. David's the worst!"

Amy shook her head. "Don't blame them. In the end it's your responsibility. It's your house and your job to make sure you leave it neat. If he's a slob, you need to nag him to clean up after himself, or you have to do it for him. Who knows? Maybe he'll listen to you where he won't listen to his parents."

Josh laughed. "He doesn't listen to anyone, believe me!"

"Okay, but you can be a good example for him. It might rub off one day."

Josh looked doubtful. "Not in my lifetime."

Amy laughed, but then looked serious. "Either way, I can't do everything by myself."

Josh nodded. "I know, Mom, you do tons, and I'm sorry. I'll do better, I promise." He turned away. "I'm going to go shower and change. By the way—what's for dinner?" He jumped out of range and laughed as Amy pretended to punch him.

"So now I'm your personal chef too?" She grinned at him. "It's lucky for you that I love cooking so much. There are potatoes baking and I figured we'd have burgers on the grill."

"Sounds great! I'll be out in 10 minutes to cook the burgers."

"Good. Get going. I want to tell you some fun news over dinner."

Ten minutes later, Josh entered the kitchen in fresh clothes, hair slicked back and smelling of soap and teenage boy. He grabbed the plate of raw burgers and the spatula and was gone again, whistling softly under his breath. Amy smiled to herself, feeling very lucky to have such a nice son. He had been unhappy when she and Jim broke up, but in the end she had known that she could not continue to live with Jim, even for Josh's sake.

Her mind drifted back to those early days. Her gorgeous Jim, who had swept her off her feet. So handsome, so tall and strong. She had met him at the Hilton, where she was working as a waitress her senior year of high school, and he was working on a renovation project. He had graduated from high school the year before. She remembered seeing him around school her junior year, but he had his own set of friends—the "jocks" —and their paths had never crossed. The next year, walking to the restaurant each afternoon, she had noticed him watching her. One day, instead of just looking up, he had intercepted her. "Don't I know you?"

Having heard every pick-up line in the book, she looked at him skeptically, her head tilted.

He blushed. "No, I mean it. Don't you go to Rancho High School?"

"Yeah. I'm a senior. Why?" The blushing was awfully cute.

"I just graduated last year. I think I saw you around school. My name's Jim." He stuck out his hand.

She smiled as she shook his hand. "I'm Amy." She paused, then turned to walk on. "Well, nice to meet you. I've got to get to work."

"Hey, could we grab a Coke after you finish?" She had to admit he had a gorgeous face, with startlingly dark brown eyes.

"Okay," she agreed somewhat reluctantly. "I get off at 9:00."

"Great. I'll come by the restaurant."

She shook her head, knowing the abuse she would get from her co-workers if they saw him. Besides, her uniform was hideous. She could change out of it fast and meet him out front. "No, I'll meet you by the front door."

"Okay." He smiled and she noticed he had very white teeth. "We can walk over to the pizza place across the street."

"Okay." She found herself smiling back. "See you."

The dinner shift seemed especially long, and she realized she was really looking forward to seeing him again. Interesting, considering she had talked to him for all of two minutes. He wasn't the type she normally went for. She generally liked the "bad boys," with their aura of excitement. The problem, of course, was that they were often very boring once you got over that first excitement of getting their attention and tried to have any kind of conversation with them.

Jim was certainly good-looking and seemed nice. She smiled, thinking about that blush. Funny, he had almost seemed shy. With those looks, you wouldn't think he'd be shy at all. She remembered he had been on the basketball team and was something of a star. Interesting that he wasn't in college somewhere. She wondered why not.

There he was, standing outside. She looked him over more completely and had to admit that she liked what she saw. Tall, light brown hair, very athletic build from his work. His jeans were worn, but clean, and he had a blue a polo shirt. She took a deep breath and pushed open the front door. He turned as she approached and smiled that gorgeous smile at her.

"Hey."

"Hey, yourself." She found herself a little breathless as she got close to him. He must be over 6'2". She thought with delight of the heels she would be able to wear and not tower over him.

"I thought we could go over to Luigi's." He pointed across the street. "Their pizza is pretty good. I think the owner is actually Italian." He grinned again. "I mean, it seems authentic."

She smiled back. "Sounds good. Lead on!"

That first date led to many more, all of them filled with talk and laughter. She would get to work early to say "hi," and he would pick her up afterwards. It turned out he couldn't afford college, and had decided not to go deep into debt when he could join his father's construction company instead. He was learning to be a master carpenter. When she asked if he was sorry not to go to college, he replied, "I think I'd like to go one day, but this just isn't the right time. The university here offered me a basketball scholarship, but I don't think I'm good enough to play beyond college, and Mom and Dad needed the extra hands right now."

She liked that he had a strong sense of family and family values, and—unlike her usual boyfriends—she found him interesting to talk to about a variety of topics. She told him that she wanted to own her own business someday, mainly because she knew she was too stubborn and opinionated to work for anyone else. She admitted that she loved to travel, and that she had grown up here in Las Vegas, which was unusual in a town of transients. She even brought him home and introduced him to her parents, which was a first. He was shy, as she'd first guessed, and surprisingly insecure, even though he was physically attractive and smart. He confessed that through middle school he had been short and plump, and that somehow he still didn't believe the mirror when he looked at it and saw himself in his taller, slimmer version. He did want to go to college one day, as he'd told her that first night, and he wanted to become an engineer. For now, he enjoyed his job very much, and he felt sure that he would continue to work with wood as a hobby even after he got his degree.

The weeks and then the months went by, and when Amy graduated from high school in June, they moved in together. Her older sisters were not pleased, but that was Amy—she did what she wanted.

For a couple of years they kept their same jobs and lived in a little apartment, saving all they could. Jim was doing well in his father's company. Carpentry was a union job, and he was considered a skilled tradesman so the money was good. And Amy found that she could do very well working the long but lucrative weekend shifts at the hotel restaurant.

They decided that Amy should go to college first, still working part-time, and Jim would go after she finished. She got her undergraduate degree in business, and they got married the evening after her graduation. Both assumed that Jim would start college the following September, but in August Amy discovered she was pregnant. Both immediately realized when it had happened. They'd gotten carried away after a crazy party and Amy had impulsively decided, "this one time wouldn't make a difference."

There followed a heated debate, with blame flying back and forth, ending with a tearful reunion and excitement at the idea of a baby. It did mean, though, that Jim would have to put off thoughts of going to college full-time for a little longer. As a compromise, Jim started taking classes in the evenings, which unfortunately also meant less time for them to be together.

Josh was born in April and was a wonderful, happy baby, but lots more work than either of them had ever imagined. To save money on childcare, Jim took care of Josh on the weekends while Amy worked. He was a great dad, but he grew tired of being Mr. Mom every single weekend. And money was still tight. And where did all the laundry come from? Suddenly a house with a dishwasher, clothes washer, dryer and yard seemed essential.

With help from both sets of parents, they bought a small house. With two working parents, a baby to raise, and a home to maintain, the months flew by. The following fall, with the house payments and all the baby costs, they both agreed that Jim needed to keep working at his lucrative job, and once again full-time college for Jim was put on the back burner. At the same time, Jim's father fell ill and Jim was given the added responsibility of business development for the company, which meant that his evenings were now devoted to client dinners and events. Amy often found herself alone with the baby at night and she resented Jim's time away. She knew intellectually that he needed to do it, but the days that then became evenings taking care of Josh by herself were exhausting. Then she would head off to work the long weekend shifts, and resent the time she had to spend away from both Josh and Jim. There were no more evenings of conversation and laughter, and discussions were usually limited to upcoming doctors' appointments for Josh or things that needed fixing around the house.

Amy finally left the Hilton and working weekends when she was offered a job processing medical claims. With Josh now in elementary school, she had more flexibility in setting her work hours and could take a job with a "normal" schedule. Amy hoped it would lead to the three of them spending more time together on outings to the park and going camping, which she and Jim had enjoyed early in their relationship, but Jim was spending more and time with his buddies. Amy also noticed that when he was home he seemed to be drinking more. Any attempts at conversation about Jim's business were met with short answers and long looks, and Amy felt completely cut off from that part of his life. She knew construction had become a very competitive field in recent years. The economy was booming and each new hotel seemed to feel obligated to outshine the one just before it. She worried that the size and scope of the jobs might be more than Jim could handle. She didn't know if he could compete in a high-stakes environment that had become filled with big corporations instead of small local companies that did business on a handshake.

One day, when Josh was in fourth grade, Amy turned the corner into their street and saw Jim's car in the driveway. She assumed this meant he had already picked up Josh from after-school care, but she had thought he said he had a dinner event to go to that evening. Maybe this meant they could actually have dinner together as a family. She pulled up to the front of the house and headed up the walkway. She heard male laughter and the television. Puzzled, she turned the key in the lock and walked in. Jim and three buddies were watching a movie with the volume turned up very high. They all had beers and she guessed after a quick glance that it was far from the first one for any of them. Jim looked up, startled, then gave her a goofy grin.

"Hi, honey. The boys and I got done on that casino job early and thought we'd come home and relax for a bit. Hope you don't mind?" His voice slurred at the end of the last sentence and she realized he was very drunk.

She nodded at them all. "No problem, boys," she said coolly before turning to Jim. Attempting to keep her tone casual, she asked, "Where's Josh?"

"Oh, he's in his room playing video games. He got a ride home from Jake's mom. He told me he doesn't have any homework."

Amy headed back to her bedroom to change out of her work clothes and stopped at Josh's closed door. Opening it gently, she was relieved to see him totally engrossed in whatever was on the computer screen. "What're you doing?" she asked brightly.

Josh looked up, smiling. "Hi, Mom. Jake loaned me a new game."

"What kind of game?"

"It's a treasure hunt. See? This guy is trying to find the gold coins in each room." He looked up, gesturing for her to come closer. Watching him maneuver deftly around the screen, she was thankful they had played games with him on the computer since he was very small. He was already showing an interest in numbers and puzzles.

"That looks great, but don't you have homework?"

"Nope. Mrs. Wilson said that tomorrow is a teacher's workday. What does that mean?"

"Oh, that's right. It means you get the day off from school, and the teachers get to have a day to work together to come up with more fun stuff for you guys to do! Okay, I'm going to make dinner."

"Mom, why does Dad have the TV up so loud? You never let me do that."

"I know, Josh. I think one of his friends must have a hard time hearing." It sounded weak to her, but Josh just nodded.

"Oh. That's like Jake's granddad. You have to yell when you talk to him."

"Exactly. Why don't you just keep playing in here until dinner? That way Dad and his friends can finish watching their show."

"Okay." He turned back to the screen and she could see he was completely involved with it again. She closed the door gently.

What was going on? She changed into casual clothes and headed back to the kitchen to start dinner. Alarm bells were going off in her head, but she tried to ignore them. Maybe Jim had just had an especially bad day. She would try to be patient and wait until his friends left before confronting him about it. She didn't want to create a scene in front of them or in front of Josh. She worked in the kitchen, listening with one ear to their noise and getting more and more angry. Even if he had a bad day, there was no excuse for drinking like that. Thank God Jake's mom had brought Josh home from the after-school program, since that was normally Jim's job. *How dare he?* She put Josh's dinner and her dinner on trays and carried them back to his room.

"Guess what? I've decided since you have no homework and no school tomorrow, we'll celebrate by having a picnic in here! Let's pretend we are in that castle with your hero."

Josh's eyes lit up. "Cool! How about Dad? Is he going to come on our adventure, too?"

"Not this time. He still has friends here, so we'll go on our adventure without him and he'll just have to come next time. Okay?"

"Okay." He turned toward the screen. "Here's the big hall where the king holds all of his big dinners. We'll pretend we are eating there."

"Great! I always wanted to eat in a castle." They toasted their glasses of milk and Josh continued making up his adventure story. Amy smiled while keeping half of her attention on the noise in the front room.

After a leisurely picnic, she got Josh ready for bed before carrying the trays back to the kitchen. Jim sauntered in just as she finished putting everything into the dishwasher. His dinner plate sat alone on the counter, the food on it cold and congealed.

"Hey baby. We're alone." He came around the counter and put his arm around her. His breath smelled overwhelmingly of beer and she pulled away.

"You smell disgusting. What in the hell are you doing, getting drunk in the middle of the week? What were you thinking?" Her questions came fast and furious and she glared at him.

His sloppy smile disappeared and he quickly became angry himself. "Well, you don't always have to be such a hardass. A guy can drink in his own house, can't he? And watch a movie with his buddies?"

"But what about Josh? You know it's your job to pick him up from school at 5:30. Thank God Jake's mom decided to bring him home!"

He stepped back and sat down with a plop on the nearest chair. "Yeah, I know." Suddenly his bravado vanished. He looked bleak. After a tense silence he said, "You know that job that I told you we won—the casino that was taking up so much time? We didn't win it. That big company from California did. Another job came up and we put together a *great* proposal for that one...." His voice faded. "But we didn't get that one, either. So the boys and I were just taking a break and drowning our sorrows." He looked so sad that she softened her tone slightly, though she was still very angry.

"There was no excuse for what you did today. Being an idiot has consequences beyond your stupidity. Today it could have affected Josh and I *will not* tolerate that." She paused. "There will be other jobs."

He bent his head further, not meeting her eyes. "I don't know if there will be other jobs. These big outfits come from all over the country. They hire the best workers because they can pay more. We've lost at least ten guys, and we lost four big jobs in the last month."

Amy felt dread seep through her system. This was obviously a bigger problem than she'd imagined. "So what *is* the next step?" She was trying to think logically, but he was still drunk. He got angry again.

"Why don't you tell me?" He staggered up and headed back toward the bathroom. "I'm going to take a shower and go to bed." She heard him bounce off of a wall and then grunt in response. She figured she would go knock on the door of the bathroom if he didn't come out in ten minutes.

A few minutes later, she was relieved to hear him emerge from the bathroom and then go into their bedroom and close the door. She threw out his uneaten dinner and started cleaning the kitchen counters a little too vigorously. Her thoughts were whirling. If Jim's company had lost four jobs in the last month, that really was serious. The networking and the client events apparently were not paying off. With a chill, she realized she had always taken for granted that the construction business would continue to do well, and she had looked at Jim's job as the steady, dependable one. Jim had not spoken about any layoffs, so she had assumed that his company had continued winning their share of the contracts. Amy knew that laying people off would start a cycle of either less work or smaller jobs, neither of which was something she liked to think about.

She shook her head and went to check on him. He was lying on his back, snoring loudly, so apparently he was still among the living. "He is really going to be hurting tomorrow," she thought, as she quietly backed out of the room.

****

"All done, Mom. Don't these burgers smell great?" Josh breezed back into the kitchen, bringing her out of her thoughts.

"Those look awesome! I'll meet you in the dining room."

Once they were both seated and the drinks were poured, she looked at Josh. "You know how all your aunts have been coming to help Grandma through her chemo weekends?" At his nod, she continued. "Well, we sisters have decided it's time we all took a trip together."

"That's a great idea, Mom. Where?"

"That's the fun part, and you are never going to believe it. Paris!" Amy beamed with excitement.

Josh paused, with a confused look, then said, "As in France?"

"Exactly."

"That is way cool, Mom! Wow, have you ever been there?"

"Nope, but Aunt Margot has an apartment there, so we are all going to hang out there for five days."

"What about me?" His look said that he was worried. He didn't say so, but he clearly did not want to be sent to his father's house for five days.

"I asked Aunt Jeannie if she could come. Then you won't have to miss any basketball and you can still have friends over."

"That sounds great, Mom. I can put up with Jason for five days. When do you plan to go?"

"In about a month."

Josh nodded. "I'll think about things Aunt Jeannie and I can cook together. And I promise I'll be better about putting the dishes in the dishwasher." He had such an earnest expression that Amy reached over and gave him a big hug. He let her hold on longer than usual and she kissed his cheek. Where would she be without her only child? They had been through so much together, and she had never been so far away from him for so long. For a minute she almost lost her nerve, and she felt a lump in her throat. To stop herself from crying, she said, "I've got an idea. Why don't we go out for an ice cream sundae and come back to the dishes?"

Josh pretended to be horrified. "But I can't leave a mess!" With a smile, Amy went to get her car keys. The dishes weren't going anywhere.

****

Amy came back to the present with a start as her pocket buzzed. Pulling her phone out, she smiled. "Things good here. Jason is a pain. Basketball practice in an hour. Love U."

She typed a quick response as she walked. "Glad you're ok. Jason worships U! Be good. Love U."

"Ha! Have fun."

She put her phone away and decided that was exactly what she would do! Who knew what adventures were waiting? Maybe she could find her own hero with a castle and gold coins! She was in France, after all!

Chapter 12. Carol

Ever since they had stopped to look in the jewelry store window, Amy had been lost in thought. Margot and Sophie were leading the way, so Carol didn't even take out her map of Paris. She figured later on she would retrace their route on the map with Margot. For now, she was content to follow along and take in the sights, sounds and smells of this different world. Each store window was unique and, as Margot had said, all beautifully presented. And the stores seemed so tiny! She couldn't imagine how they stayed in business.

Next to the jewelry store was a shop window filled with beautiful scarves, and next to that a window with two male mannequins in slim, tailored suits. Long legs below a form-fitting jacket and a bright purple tie with a striped shirt underneath. What sort of man could ever pull off that look? Certainly no American man that she knew! The whole look was somehow petite, which was not a word that she had ever thought of to describe a man. Maybe that was just how the men were built here. She had noticed at the airport that the *gendarmes* at the customs area all seemed to be more compact, somehow, than American men. She shook herself. What was she doing focusing so much on how the men looked, for heaven's sake? Looking across the street, she noticed a café with couples sitting next to one another, watching the world go by. She hoped she and her sisters would stop to do some of that. It was all a bit much to take in.

Carol got a face full of cigarette smoke from a group of teenagers passing by. Then she noticed a hint of lavender perfume from a well-dressed older woman. They passed a couple of workers coming out of an entryway covered in what looked like plaster dust and she caught a whiff of body odor.

They rounded a corner and walked into a spring breeze. Carol put on her sweater, glad she had remembered to pack it. She looked around, wanting to pinch herself to make sure it was real, and willing herself to believe she was actually in Paris, France. She felt lighter, somehow, and carefree. What a difference from thirty-six hours before....

****

Carol opened the door to the house slowly, listening to see if she could tell who was where and what kind of mood everyone was in. Silence. "Good," she thought. "I can get started on my packing without an audience."

Heading straight up the stairs, she dumped her purse and sweater on the bed and pulled her bag out of the back of her closet. Opening it on the bed, she found two pairs of her daughter's underwear left from the last trip. "From when and where?" she wondered. "Oh, that's right. Spring break and college visits." They had gone out to Ohio and looked at several schools in the Midwest of different sizes to give Gwen some sense of what she might be interested in. So far, all they'd figured out was that Gwen didn't like really small schools and didn't like Ohio.

Carol turned to the dresser and started pulling out her own socks and underwear, thinking about what the weather would be in Paris, and about Margot's comment about "not standing out." Carol knew that of all her sisters, she was the most conservative dresser, so whatever she chose, she would blend in better than Amy or Sophie. She pulled the bottom drawer out to look at pants, then jumped when a voice spoke behind her.

"Oh! You startled me," she said to George. He moved to the other side of the bed and she continued. "I didn't hear anyone when I came in, so I assumed you were out."

"I was in the basement, so I didn't hear you either. I came up for a paper I needed."

They both fell silent, and she had a moment to really look at George. He had aged during the last couple of years. His brown hair was now flecked with gray and the lines on his face were deeper. He had really gained weight too, she realized. This last couple of years, his only exercise had been walking the dog, and it showed.

He looked at her for a moment, and then spoke quietly. "Do you really have to go?"

She paused. "Yes. I think it's a good idea for a couple of reasons. First, I haven't seen my sisters in a very long time. We all agreed we should get together." She paused. "And you know the second reason. I think it's a good idea for us to be apart for a few days. I need some time on my own to think about us—about where we go from here."

George nodded slowly. "Carol, I just want you to know, I honestly had no idea you were so unhappy these last months and I am trying hard to figure out how to fix it."

"Years, George," she corrected gently. "I don't know if it can be fixed anymore. Being so unhappy for so long has made me basically shut down my heart, and I don't know what I'm going to find when I open it again." A look of pain crossed his face. "I know that's hard for you to hear, but I think it's about time we were honest with each other. That, for me, has to be the first step, and then we can see what comes next."

He nodded, choked briefly, then started again. "Intellectually, I understand all that, but emotionally, it's killing me." He stopped, unable to go on.

She almost went to his side, but stopped herself. She had felt bad for him for years, but it wasn't solving the problem. Every time they tried to talk he would act miserable, she would feel guilty, and she would relent, burying their problems and making her feel that, once again, she had "given in" and lost something in the process. "We will talk about it when I get back."

He walked to the door, then turned. "I'll see you downstairs. I'd like to go over the kids' schedules one more time, if that's okay."

"Sure, I'll be right down." She waited until he had closed the bedroom door, then sat down on the edge of the bed holding her stomach. Why did conversations with him always leave her feeling like she was the bad guy? She felt the familiar ache and rubbed her stomach, afraid that she was getting an ulcer.

Looking back at their first few years, she remembered how they had been so close, so energized by each other. He had been a political activist and was always working on one campaign or another. Sometimes he was paid and sometimes he wasn't, but Carol made enough money for them to get by. When asked, Carol would say he was a "campaign consultant," which was basically true, and certainly believable because he loved to argue politics. They would have heated discussions about whatever the relevant topic of the day was, and somehow they always ended up in bed, where the conversation would continue, with lots of laughter and debate. It hadn't mattered where they each stood on each topic. They just had so much fun arguing and stretching their brains to find facts to support their views. Then Gwen had come along, and their energy was rechanneled and refocused on a newborn who slept for twenty minutes at a time and never seemed happy when she was awake.

Things had gotten easier when Gwen turned two, but then Brian arrived and the cycle started all over again. This time it was both easier and harder: easier because he was a smiling, happy baby, but harder because it was now twice the work and twice the expense. Neither Carol nor George felt they could ever take a break. Carol's responsibilities at her job started increasing, but working for a non-profit organization was not a way to get rich. They agreed George needed to find a steady job.

But somehow, no job was good enough. This one was boring, that one was in support of a bad cause, and so on. A year passed, then three, and George continued to "look," but slowly the number of interviews lessened, and his Sunday review of the want ads and his online job searches became playtime with the kids. Now when people asked, Carol shortened his job to "consultant."

It wasn't all bad. In those early years, he was great with the kids, they didn't have to pay for childcare, and it had been nice to have him at home so that she didn't have to rush out of the office every day at 5:00. Unfortunately, George wasn't big on cooking, or cleaning, or laundry, though he did manage the checkbook and daily chores like grocery shopping. Money was always tight, but he seemed to budget wisely and there seemed to be enough for an occasional movie date or video game for the kids.

Everything changed one day when Carol was doing her weekend cleaning. In moving a pile of unopened mail on his desk, she noticed several bills. On impulse, she opened three from credit card companies and her heart stopped. $30,000! $25,000!

And $20,000! How could they be in so much debt? She had to read the bills again, and then again. How long had they been $75,000 in debt? She felt her stomach clench with nausea.

She found George sitting in front of the television, and in a strained voice asked him if they could talk in his office. When she confronted him, he looked at her with mild surprise and asked if she really thought that what she made was enough for them to live on. "Everyone has debt, honey. What's the big deal?"

Appalled, she just stared at him. Her normal calm left her and she felt an anger welling up that she had never known. *"What? Are you serious?* We can't live like this! 'Everyone' does *not* have debt— at least not like this! We have to figure out how to pay it off!" She stormed out of the room, shaking with emotion. Her confidence was shattered. Who was this person that she had entrusted to manage her finances, and how could he possibly think that $75,000 of debt was acceptable?

She realized her anger and frustration were directed at herself as much as at him, for blindly trusting him to handle their money. How stupid could she be, letting him pay the bills all these years? Why had she never questioned the fact that there always seemed to be enough money?

She thought back to all the times she had come home from work, exhausted, to find dishes piled in the sink; papers, magazines and toys scattered throughout the house; and three hungry people looking at her asking what was for dinner. She always pushed through her fatigue, believing it was her job to cook and clean while George took care of the kids, shopped, and managed the bills. And now it turned out they were enormously in debt!

Resolved, she marched back to where he was sitting at his desk.

"This debt is absolutely unacceptable. I take partial responsibility for not questioning you more closely on your oversight of our finances and spending. I can't believe you honestly assume that 'everyone' has debt and so, somehow, it's 'okay,' but I've learned something about you today that I will *never* forget."

"The first step we are going to take is that *you* are going to get a job. I don't care if you are working the counter at McDonald's; you *will* have a job in the next sixty days."

"The second step is I'm going to go to the bank to see if we can refinance the mortgage and pay off some of this debt. I hope you realize that you have seriously reduced the number of colleges that your children can consider, and made it impossible for them to leave college without having loans to pay back?"

George looked puzzled. "I never assumed we would pay for college for our kids. My parents didn't pay for mine. Why would I pay for theirs?"

Carol stumbled backward into a chair. Who *was* this man? Could this really be the man she had married? All of that talking in the early days of their marriage and they had never had this conversation? How could she have been so clueless about how he viewed money and about his priorities for spending it? What signs had she missed?

She took a deep breath to slow her heart. "It's obvious that I've been making assumptions based on my own upbringing. I know you had a rough childhood, but I thought it had made you want *more* for *your* kids."

"I do want more, but I like to think I'm a realist. We haven't been able to put much money away, so what money we have been able to save has been put into your retirement account. That seemed like the first priority to me. College loans are cheap."

Carol spoke again, more quietly. "It's now obvious to me that we have some big differences of opinion on some major life issues. But that doesn't change the current situation, which I view as *very* serious." She suddenly felt overwhelmed and exhausted. "I'm going to bed. Monday, we start trying to fix this." She walked slowly toward the door, pausing on the threshold to look back at George. He was sitting with a stunned and uncomprehending look on his face.

Carol took over the checkbook and refinanced the mortgage. George started looking for a job. They also started going to counseling. It was an expense that Carol was willing to pay to get her marriage and her life back. But George didn't think the counseling sessions were helpful and said so loudly and often in front of Gwen and Brian. He insisted that he was trying to find work, but week after week went by and he was still at home. He took the kids where they needed to go, which by middle school was a part-time job in itself, but Carol wondered what he did with his time all day. He did start attending the neighborhood association meetings two evenings a month, and Carol hoped the connections he made would lead to a job. But the months, and then the years, went by, and he was still at home. In every conversation she had with him, she tried to start with something positive, but it always ended with questions about his unsuccessful job search. The sixty days to find a job became sixty months, and every time she resolved to confront him on it, he came home with a "lead," or was especially nice to the kids, or seemed especially sincere about changing, and her resolve crumbled. There also always seemed to be a child nearby, which made frank discussion difficult because she didn't want to involve or worry them.

Carol had to admit to herself that she also contributed to the situation because she didn't like confrontation, plain and simple. She never had. She had often been the mediator between her sisters growing up, but she preferred to catch disagreements early, before the anger and drama had a chance to escalate. After her "sixty days" ultimatum, she hadn't done anything to show she meant it, and George quickly caught on.

In the end, the avoidance was as exhausting as the confrontation and recent events had brought Carol to a crossroads in her own mind. She hoped this trip would give her the emotional distance she needed to come up with some answers. She was at the point where she had absolutely nothing to say to George. She felt dried up and empty inside.

What was she going to do?

****

"Anyone ready for something to drink and eat?" Margot's voice interrupted Carol's thoughts. "I know just the place!" They rounded a corner and stopped at the entrance to one of the most beautiful squares Carol had ever seen. Carol shook herself, setting all thoughts aside. She breathed deeply, smelling the roses in the garden, the scent of coffee from the café, and a slight mustiness from the antiques shop door to her left. Enough introspection. Time to live life!

Chapter 13. Margot

"What do you think?" I could see from all of their faces that this had been a good choice.

"Wow!" said Carol in a delighted tone.

"It's called the *Place des Vosges*. Henry IV had it built in 1605 as the city residence for the royal court. It's had a checkered career over the years, though. The Marais area, in general, fell out of favor for awhile and many buildings became rundown. But now it's on the upswing. Throughout history there have been interesting people who have lived in this square. Victor Hugo, for instance, who wrote *Les Miserables* and the *Hunchback of Notre Dame*, and Cardinal Richelieu during the French Revolution."

A steady stream of busy Parisians passed us as my sisters gawked at the scene. There were people with strollers, several dogs playing chase on the gravel path, and a young couple lying on the grass, oblivious to all of the activity around them. There was a fountain in the center and several children had small boats they were floating along the edges.

"To be honest, I love it here because it's such a great people-watching spot. Let's go over to that café with the tables in the sun."

The four of us sat down. "You'll notice that most couples sit next to each other at these tables looking out, rather than sitting across from each other, the way we do at home. That way both people can watch all the action. With four of us, it's a little more complicated!"

Amy laughed. "I want an outside seat! If there's a handsome Frenchman out there he can come sit next to me. "

I laughed, but Sophie and Carol rolled their eyes.

We all ordered coffee, Amy ordered her *Coca Light*, and we sat in silence for a moment, watching the people flowing by.

"Where are all these people going?" Carol asked. "And why aren't they at work? It's Friday afternoon, after all."

"Some are tourists, like us. Some are students. Some could be on their way to meetings. I know the French start work later, and I think they work later into the evening too. Generally they have a more relaxed lifestyle than at home, and personally, I love that. Each time I come, I get off the plane and can feel myself slowing down. The French are marvelous at really experiencing life. It's in their genes. They will have a five-course meal and appreciate every bite without once looking at their watches. I think their priorities are good for the soul!"

Sophie nodded. "I travel so much for work that I feel like I'm always on the edge of rushing somewhere. This feels really nice to just enjoy the moment." She smiled and looked around at all of us. "You know the other funny thing? For me, the relaxation thing goes deeper. It's not just a control thing—that is, having to slow down and just let Margot tell me what to do." She grinned at me. "Seriously, since we've gotten here, I've felt myself relaxing more completely than I have for a long time. I first noticed it sitting in Margot's living room. It's not just Paris, it's being with you guys, people I can be completely myself with." She looked sad suddenly. "I hadn't realized it until I got here, but to be honest, I can't remember the last time I just relaxed." She lapsed into silence.

Carol spoke up. "You mean at work?"

Sophie nodded. "Definitely at work. Even with Joan, my best friend, I am always a little on edge, always thinking about my reputation, what people think of me, the right thing to say, stuff like that."

Amy nodded. "I think everyone feels that way at work, especially if you're looked at as a leader and if you're moving up in the food chain the way you are! But what about at home? With Roger?"

Sophie sighed. "It's hard to say out loud, but if I'm being honest—and I've decided this trip for me is all about honesty—no, I don't think I ever truly relax at home, even with Roger. I don't know… somehow there is always a tension, a little 'being on my best behavior' feeling."

"Really?" Amy looked thoughtful. "Why do you think that is?"

"I don't know. It was never like that at the beginning, but now there are so many things going on all the time—the kids and their schedules, my travel schedule, my work schedule…. I feel like I'm always multi-tasking and my thoughts are somewhere else, planning the next day and the next week and how to get it all done. So even when I'm home, I'm not really there. I'm worrying about the next meeting or trip." Sophie paused. "It's exhausting, frankly."

Carol was now nodding vigorously. "That's exactly how it is for me. And why is it that we seem to be the ones who have to make all the decisions, and somehow have all the responsibility for everything? Keeping everyone's schedules straight, getting kids to the doctor, scheduling all house repairs. Even the dumb stuff, like making sure everybody has socks that fit and there's enough dog food for the week. Only moms do those things."

Amy laughed. "I feel like that, but figured a big part of it is being divorced. I don't have another adult in the equation to shoulder some of the burden."

Sophie said, "It must be really brutal for you! For me, at least Roger is the shuttle bus service for practices, and he keeps everything organized on the home front. You know what a neat freak he is—and he's a good cook, too. So I really don't have to sweat the daily tasks. It's the big picture stuff, knowing when all of our various kinds of doctors' appointments are supposed to happen, remembering when to check in with teachers at school, setting up appointments with the accountant or furnace repairman or dog groomer... stuff that affects our life, but can get forgotten in the everyday craziness."

I spoke up at this point. "It sounds like we all have the ultimate responsibility for our households. Sometimes I just feel like I can't do it all anymore. The other day, I stopped sorting laundry while discussing doctors' appointments with Paul, and it was one more case of Paul being completely oblivious. I said to him, 'What if I got hit by a bus?

Would you ever be able to remember that the boys need to go to the dentist every six months? Or that summer camp registrations are due in March? All these things that are rolling around in my head all the time?' He just looked at me with this blank look of 'What am I doing wrong?' And honestly, I just had to start laughing—because if I didn't, I would start screaming and it's not worth getting ulcers over."

Carol looked sad. "They just have a different kind of brain, I guess. It can drive you over the edge, for sure."

Amy said, "I know that, now Josh is older, I lean on him, probably more than I should. Sophie has Roger at home. Margot and Paul both work full time, so they pay someone to clean every other week and bring in dinner a lot. Is that fair, Margot?"

I nodded ruefully. "I hate to admit it, but you've described us pretty well. Or there are days we just have pancakes for dinner!"

Amy turned back to Carol. "So what about you? With George doing consulting, does that mean he has time to take on some of that home front stuff?"

Carol was silent and the three of us watched her, waiting for her response. She was looking at her hands. I thought I saw her turn her wedding band on her finger. She finally looked up at all of us.

"Well... that's an interesting question." She sighed. "This is hard, but my answer goes back to Sophie's point about honesty." She took a deep breath. "Actually, George isn't a consultant. In fact, he hasn't had a real job since Gwen was born."

There was a stunned silence. Amy was the first to speak. "Wait. Are you saying that he hasn't had a job in, what, sixteen years? Is he a stay-at-home dad like Roger? How do you get by on your salary alone?"

Carol saw Amy's look of alarm and cast down her eyes again. "At our house, George is great with the kids, but not so great on the cleaning or cooking fronts." She paused, and then continued. "He had just finished working on a political campaign when Gwen was born, and as you guys may recall, she was a tough baby. He took care of her at night so I could sleep and be coherent at work the next day. Then Brian was born, and two is more than twice the work, right?" Margot and Sophie both nodded. "It was great to have him home to take care of the little ones, because work for me was getting more and more stressful. To earn more money, I had to make my way up the corporate ladder, doing all the right things and showing what a hard worker I was. When both kids were in preschool, George started his job search again. But somehow, no job was good enough for him. This one was not challenging enough, or that one had the wrong politics. Over time, he seemed to be searching less and less, and I just got tired of asking about it all the time." She fell silent.

I spoke up. "Why didn't he take on the meals and cleaning at that point? If he wasn't working and bringing in money, didn't he take over those things for you?"

Carol appeared overwhelmed with emotion. "Somehow, that didn't compute. There is an old-fashioned part of him, I guess, that still thinks of those tasks as women's work. When I get home in the evening, I have to cook dinner and clean the house."

Amy looked furious. "What? That's ridiculous! If he's not making money, he needs to be doing everything else! So what *does* he do? Sit on his ass?" She looked ready to jump over the ocean and give George a piece of her mind.

Carol looked up and her eyes were filled with tears. "I haven't told you the worst part yet." A small sob shook her and she wiped her eyes before continuing. "When Gwen was ten, I found out that we had over $70,000 in debt." At their shocked looks, she added, "I don't know why I let him pay the bills. I guess it felt good that he was doing *something*, you know? Anyway, I thought somehow he was being very frugal and making it work on my salary. He wasn't. When I confronted him, I realized for the first time that I really didn't know him at all."

Amy thumped her fist on the table so hard that everyone jumped. "What happened after you found out?"

"I refinanced the house and told him he had to get a job."

"And?" Amy's glare bored into Carol, who squirmed in her seat.

"He always finds ways to avoid talking about it, and no, he hasn't gotten a job yet. He uses the kids as shields, because he knows I won't talk about things like this in front of them. We started going to counseling, but he hated it. I still wanted to make it work. I didn't want to fail."

Tears were rolling down her face now. "Then, last month, I found a credit card bill hidden behind the couch for a card I didn't recognize. In his name. When I opened the envelope, I found out he owes $35,000 on it." She looked at Amy. "I just stood there for a minute. I honestly didn't feel a thing. It was like my emotions had all been drained out of me. When I went to ask him about it, I almost felt like it wasn't me standing there—that, instead, I was watching the whole scene play out below me. Anyway, it turns out that he's been gambling. He goes to a horse racetrack called Arlington Park.

Carol paused. "This trip, and my hope that I could talk to you all about this, was the only thing that has kept me sane these last couple of weeks."

"You've got to kick him out!" Amy was enraged. Sophie gave her a sharp look and put her arm around Carol's shoulders.

"I know that seems like the obvious immediate first step. But I don't know if I can afford to do that. We can't even afford one household. How are we going to support two?"

"Why do *you* have to support two?" Amy's eyes were blazing. "Why can't you just kick his ass out?"

Carol looked frustrated. "It's complicated. I'm talking to an attorney now, but keep in mind I've been supporting him for years. He could make an argument that he stayed home to take care of the kids and I need to continue to support him. Like a housewife who stays home for years and then needs assistance while trying to get a job. It looks the same from the outside, if he plays it right."

"That is bullshit!" Amy was silent for a moment. "But I guess I can see how the courts might see it that way. This is *crazy!*"

Carol nodded. "The whole thing has been a nightmare that I can't escape. I haven't talked to anyone about this except the lawyer." She looked around. "I don't even admit to my friends and colleagues that he isn't working, so I'm certainly not going to talk about the whole gambling thing. It makes me feel like a failure."

The more I thought about my sister supporting a healthy, able-bodied man, the angrier I got. "Carol, *you* are not the failure here. You can't just sit back and put up with this crap."

She looked miserable. "I know." She added quietly. "It's just really hard to talk about. George gets angry and storms out of the house, and it scares the kids. I know he adores them and he *says* he loves me. Then he acts repentant and sad when he comes back." She paused. "It's a cycle we've been through again and again."

She continued. "That's why taking this trip was so critical. I knew I needed to talk about the whole situation and get some feedback, and you all are the perfect audience. I told him before I left that I was taking this trip not only for our reunion, but also to figure out what I was going to do."

Amy muttered, "I bet that scared him! Look at his nice, comfy life. He does *not* want to lose that!"

Everyone fell silent for a moment and I reached over and squeezed Carol's hand. "We're all here for you. I hope you know that."

She smiled. "I do now." After a silence, she said, "Well, that's *my* dirty laundry." She heaved a giant sigh. "I can't believe how much better I feel just saying it out loud. I want to hear ideas from you over these next few days. I need your help to get through this."

Amy now grabbed her hand. "I hope you don't think you're the only one with laundry. I've got my own issues. I bet we all do." Sophie and I nodded.

I said, "The first step to finding solutions to problems is admitting they exist, right?" Everyone nodded and we raised our glasses in a toast. "To honesty, revelations, and solutions. Agreed?"

"Agreed," everyone chimed in together. Carol's confession about her problems made me feel it was going to be easier for me to reveal mine. Now I just had to find the right moment . . . .

Chapter 14. Carol

Carol sat quietly, feeling drained but also relieved. It had felt so good to say out loud what had been on her mind for so long, and she felt blessed to have these women who knew her so well and who would support her. Margot paid the bill and they started gathering their belongings. Carol felt stiff, but much less foggy after the coffee break. Grabbing her purse, she followed Margot around the tables and out into the street.

"We'll go up that way." Margot pointed to the right. "The bus stop is just outside the square, and I figure we've walked enough this afternoon."

Amy nodded. "Amen to that!"

Carol, glancing ahead, noticed a man standing next to some small pictures by the archway through which Margot was headed. As they got closer the pictures came into focus, and she was drawn to their strong, broad strokes and muted colors. They were paintings of what she would call "glimpses" of Paris. One was a storefront filled with delicious-looking breads; another was an archway and, tucked just inside it, a beautiful wooden door that seemed to glow, lit by the beams of a setting sun. She asked everyone to wait and moved closer to the pictures. One showed a young girl standing on a balcony that seemed to be attached to the edge of the sloping roof. Perhaps those were smaller rooms at the top of the building; they seemed to be in the eaves themselves. The sun was setting and the outline of the building behind the girl stood out starkly against the sky. She was gazing out with a look that seemed to be both frightened and excited. She was dressed simply, in clothes that looked worn but neat, and Carol was struck by how much story was behind the simple picture. She found herself imagining a whole life. A student, perhaps, embarking on some new adventure? Or a young woman starting a new job?

Amy had gotten distracted by another shop, and Sophie and Margot stood at a distance, looking at the pictures and chatting, leaving Carol to her thoughts.

"You like it?" A soft voice with a heavy French accent spoke behind her.

She jumped. She had forgotten all about the man standing there.

"Yes, very much." She smiled at him, then turned back to the picture. "Did you paint this?"

"*Oui.*"

She looked more closely at the painting. "It's so realistic." He said nothing, and she stammered, "Oh, I'm so sorry—I don't speak French."

He smiled. "I speak a little English."

"These pictures are beautiful!" Carol exclaimed.

"And so are you, *Mademoiselle.*"

His flattery was ridiculous, but she blushed anyway.

"That is *Madame*... but thank you very much. To me, these pictures look like memories that have been painted."

He nodded. "You are correct. These were all painted from pictures in my mind of places that I have known in my life. I paint what I see around me."

She nodded. "They're not just pretty pictures of buildings. They give a glimpse of the life going on inside."

He extended his hand to her. "*Merci, Madame.* Allow me to introduce myself. My name is Jean-Michel Moreau."

She shook his hand, noticing that his grasp was warm and firm. "My name is Carol. Carol Jamison." Jean-Michel had brown eyes that seemed amused. She wondered what he was thinking. A dormant part of her brain stirred. It had been years since she'd been curious about a man. How had such a talented painter ended up selling his paintings by an archway in the square? She found herself reluctant to let go of his hand.

"You are perhaps wondering why I am here, selling my art to *touristes?*"

Carol blushed again. He had read her mind.

He continued, "I was a teacher for many years, but my painting kept calling to me, so I decided to change my life."

She nodded. "You 're lucky—to do what you really want to do."

"It is not luck, *Madame*," he disagreed politely. "I think each of us should find that thing that is special to us and we should do that. We only have one life, and it is short. We should not waste a moment of it."

She thought she detected sorrow in his eyes, but she was afraid to meet his look. Then she felt foolish. He was just a street painter!

"May I ask how much this painting is?" She pointed toward the young girl.

"For you, 120 euros."

She calculated quickly and figured it was about $160. She felt a tug as she looked at the picture. Somehow the young girl reminded her of herself, and the painting made her remember how excited and scared she had been when starting her first job. The painting was full of young energy and nervous tension. She liked the idea of having it in her office, to remind herself of both this trip and of her own dreams—whatever they were. Maybe it was time to dust them off, and this picture would make sure she did so, even after she returned home.

She smiled brightly at Jean-Michel. "I'll take it."

He smiled in return and bowed slightly. "*Merci, Madame.* That is very kind. I hope it will bring you joy and good memories of Paris. Allow me to wrap it for you." He walked over next to the wall and pulled out some brown paper and tape, which gave her a chance to look at him without being observed. He was slim and only slightly taller than she was, with thick black hair that was turning to grey at the temples. At this point, her sisters realized what was happening and all crowded over to see what she had bought before he wrapped it up. He looked around at the group in surprise and gave the women a big smile. "Who are these beautiful ladies?"

Amy smiled broadly. "Her sisters. I'm Amy, that is Sophie, and that is Margot."

He shook hands with each, looking them squarely in the eye. "*Quatre* sisters? May I ask what you are doing in Paris?"

Carol spoke first. "We're having a reunion!"

He looked pleased. "In France, we value family very highly. I am happy for you that you are spending some time together."

Carol said. "We are just starting to realize how important it is to stay in touch." Her sisters all nodded. She added impulsively, "We live far apart, and had all become very involved in our daily lives." She blushed again, wondering why she was telling this man her life story.

Jean-Michel nodded in understanding. "Your country is very large, and I think your culture is one of exploration and adventure, so your young people leave home and go seek their fortune far from home."

"I think there's some truth to that." Carol loved the poetic way he expressed himself. Jean-Michel finished wrapping the picture and put a string around it, creating a handle for Carol to carry it.

"*Mesdames*, it is six o'clock and time for me to stop selling paintings for the day. May I ask you to join me for an *aperitif*? It is customary to have a drink at this time of day." He pointed to a café on the other side of the archway.

There was a moment of silence before Margot spoke up. "If no one needs to get back to the apartment, we could have a drink and then go straight to the restaurant?"

Everyone murmured in agreement and Carol shot Margot a grateful glance. She turned back to Jean-Michel. "I hope you will not regret inviting four loud American women to join you." She laughed easily, and felt a little giddy. This was not her usual behavior.

He smiled back warmly, then took her hand and kissed it. "I would be most honored to repay your kindness to me. Please, go over to the café and I will join you after I finish packing up my things." His glance was warm, almost a caress.

"See you there," Carol said a little breathlessly.

The four women found two tables next to each other and once again arranged themselves in a row facing the street. The sun had moved further toward the horizon and the shadows were advancing across the far side of the square. At the cafes scattered around the square, couples were finding their spots, while families gathered their things and herded whining children toward a row of parked cars.

The waiter came over and Margot explained that they were waiting for a friend. Amy leaned over to Carol, who was at one end of the row, and said impishly, "He's cute."

Carol looked at her with a feigned look of innocence. "I didn't notice."

"Yeah, right. What was he telling you?"

"He said that he was a teacher before, but that he loved painting and now that's how he earns his living."

"He has such warm brown eyes. They look right into you."

Carol looked across to where Jean-Michel was packing up his paintings and turned back to Amy. "I did notice that," she confessed.

"He seems to think you're pretty cute, too."

"Oh, sure, that was just his sales technique." Carol paused. "Which worked, as you can see!"

Amy made a face. "You didn't buy that because of any sales technique. It's a really nice painting."

Carol mused, "You know, I felt a connection to it right away, and could sense a whole story behind it."

Sophie spoke. "I think the girl in the picture looks a little like a younger you."

Carol turned toward her. "Do you really? I kind of thought so too, but figured I was imagining it."

Margot said, "No, you aren't imagining it. There was a definite resemblance."

Carol said, "He did such a good job of catching her excitement and tension about something." She stopped and looked sheepish. "At least, that's what I saw."

Sophie agreed. "Absolutely. He's a talented guy." She paused. "With an eye for beauty." She looked affectionately at Carol.

"Don't give me that. I'm just an old has-been."

Sophie said indignantly, "No you're not, Carol. Don't *ever* let yourself think that. You're a very attractive woman. I mean it!" she said, when Carol started shaking her head vigorously. "You need to believe that. You *are* attractive, and you're also one of the most generous, giving people I know. I'm proud you're my sister."

Margot jumped in. "Me, too! That's why we need to figure out this George thing before you head back."

Carol gazed across at Jean-Michel. "Thank you for saying that. I admit I could use a little flattery right now."

Amy teased, "Jean-Michel seems to excel at that."

Jean-Michel joined them, seating himself next to Carol. The waiter handed out menus, and Margot said, "Wine or beer are your two best choices at a café like this. They aren't into mixed drinks the way we are at home. If you want wine, we can order a *pichet*, which is a little carafe that has two to three glasses in it. For the beer, you can get 25, 50 or 100 centiliters. I recommend one of the first two —the 100 is a huge mug of beer." She turned to Amy. "You could probably handle it, baby sister, but you may not want to try on top of any jet lag you may have going on. We were going to take a nap before dinner, remember?"

Amy laughed. "Okay, maybe next time. I'll take a 50 cl Kronenbourg."

Sophie turned to Carol. "I think I'm more in the mood for red wine. Want to share a *pichet* with me?" She glanced at Margot to see how her pronunciation had been. Margot gave her a thumbs up.

Carol looked anxious. "Do we need to order a particular kind?"

Margot said, "You can—or you can just get the house wine, which is usually fine."

Jean-Michel had been silent to this point, but now he spoke up. "I would suggest the 2010 Macon. That was a very good year for the *Bourgogne* region." His pronunciation gave Carol a shiver. The sound was so liquid and, for her, incredibly romantic.

Ever-practical Sophie asked, "Is it expensive?"

"*Non,*" said Jean-Michel, signaling to the waiter who had been hovering just out of earshot. He quickly ordered for them and Carol was struck again by the liquid sounds that rippled together in a musical stream. She looked at her sisters and back at Jean-Michel. "That order would not have sounded nearly as good in English."

They all laughed and Jean-Michel laughed with them. "But *ecoutez.* I can do an American accent!" He was charming them all. In flat, American tones, he said "Oh, look at the painter. Do you like these pictures, Bob?"

They all laughed.

"Who's Bob?" Amy asked.

"People speak as if I am not there," Jean-Michel explained. "Unlike you, *Madame.*" He smiled at Carol, who looked shyly pleased.

He turned to the entire group. "Now, please tell me, each of you, where you are from."

Amy, Sophie, and Margot gave short, simple descriptions of where they were from and quick descriptions of their families. Margot left out the part about her apartment in order to focus on Carol, who spoke last.

"I live in Chicago."

Jean-Michel said, "Chicago. I have been there. What a wonderful city!"

Carol laughed for no reason. "I agree, but it sounds much more interesting when you say it!"

Jean-Michel smiled. "Please continue. And your family?"

Carol realized she was reluctant to reveal to this man that she was married. What was wrong with her? It wasn't like it would make any difference. "Yes, I'm married with two children."

He nodded. "How old are the children?"

"Sixteen and fourteen. A girl and a boy."

The waiter brought the drinks and there was silence as everyone took a sip. The noises around them became more noticeable: the soft murmur of conversation, the clink of glasses and plates from the bar area, an occasional honk from an unhappy driver on the nearby street.

"Now, Jean-Michel, your turn," said Carol. "Please tell us a little bit about yourself."

He smiled. "I am not interesting, but I will tell you a little. I was a teacher for many years, but when my wife died seven years ago, I decided to paint because that is truly what I love."

Carol looked at him sadly. So that was what she had seen in his eyes. "I'm sorry to hear about your wife."

Jean-Michel looked at her and smiled wearily. "Thank you. It was cancer and not expected. But," he shrugged, "it is what happened. We do not have control over some things in life."

Amy spoke up. "You're right. There are many things we cannot control in our lives. But Jean-Michel, don't you think we should control those things we can, and change them if we are unhappy?" She did not glance at Carol, but Carol knew she was asking the question for her.

Jean-Michel was silent for a moment then spoke quietly. "It is not always easy to tell what we control and what we do not control in our lives. Sometimes there are things that look easy to change, but they are connected to other things that are not easy to change." He stopped and looked apologetic. "My English is not so good. I am sorry for that. Do you understand what I am saying?"

Carol nodded and reached over to touch his hand briefly. She spoke quietly. "I think you are very wise, Jean-Michel. I agree with you. We would like things to be simple, but life doesn't always cooperate."

Jean-Michel nodded and looked deeply into her eyes. Carol, for a moment, felt like they were alone. Sounds around her muted and she looked back at him, searching for something in his eyes, but not sure what she wanted to find. He spoke. "I think you have a very complicated life right now. I do not know you at all, but I will say to you that I can see you are a very good person, and I believe that it will all work out for you as it should." He smiled gently. "You are beautiful, inside and out."

Carol felt the warmth of his words spreading gently through her and blushed again. She squeezed his hand. "Thank you." She broke her gaze and looked around at her sisters, who were all trying very hard to look at anything but the two of them. "Let's toast something." She felt flustered and desperately hoped a sister would come to her rescue.

"Great idea." Amy smiled. "Let's toast to family, and to seeing each other in a new and beautiful place, Paris."

Jean-Michel raised his glass and said, "You are all welcome to my city, and I hope you will find much to please you here."

They all touched glasses and then drank. Their toast was both joyful and melancholy. After a moment, the conversation resumed and the five of them talked about life and funny experiences until Margot looked at her watch.

"Ladies, it's eight o'clock and time for us to get going. We need to stay awake through our dinner, at least."

Jean-Michel smiled. "I am honored that you have all spent your first evening in Paris with me. I am here at this corner many days. Please feel free to come back and say hello again before your trip is finished." He reached for the bill, which was sitting on the table and waved their hands away. "Consider it my gift at the beginning of your journey."

The sisters protested, but Jean-Michel was adamant. After many handshakes and expressions of thanks, the sisters headed once more toward the corner where Margot had been directing them two hours earlier. Carol was the last to leave. She turned to Jean-Michel, who gave her the painting.

"Thank you for everything," she said. "My painting, the wine, everything."

Jean-Michel squeezed her hand. "You are most welcome. I have enjoyed very much my time with you and your sisters." He paused before adding, "I would like to say again that you are a special person, and I would be very happy for you to come visit me any time." His look made her feel attractive and desirable—which, she realized with a start, she had not felt in a long time. She did not feel threatened or uncomfortable. He was simply offering her the gift of appreciating who she was, without any strings attached. She felt warmed and somehow liberated, more alive than she had felt in a long time. She blushed again, and withdrew her hand to hug her painting to her chest. Those warm brown eyes....

Carol sighed. "Well, thank you again." She turned quickly and hurried to join her sisters, who were waiting under the archway. As she reached them, she turned one last time and waved to Jean-Michel, who returned her wave before turning away.

"Wow, that was an awesome start to our trip," breathed Amy. "First day, and we find a romantic Frenchman!"

Carol added, "And I got a wonderful painting. I hope all of you find as special a souvenir as mine."

Sophie spoke up. "Right now all I want to find is that restaurant. I'm starving!"

Margot promised a five-minute walk and, as they started off, Carol adjusted her grip on the painting. She felt light-headed and wasn't sure if she should attribute that to the wine or to Jean-Michel. Her heart pounded faster as she re-lived the conversation in her mind. She wanted to feel like this again—alive, and tingly. She promised herself she was *not* going to forget this feeling. She *was* going to change her life!

Chapter 15. Carol

Margot opened the door to the restaurant and motioned them in. It was small, just a dozen tables, each set with a white tablecloth, a candle, and a single rose. Photos hung on the walls, which were old brick, and the hardwood floors were a warm brown. A bar with dozens of bottles lined up against a huge mirror made the front of the restaurant seem open, while the rear of the room was intimate and cozy—and completely empty. The maitre d' greeted Margot. "*Bonsoir, Madame.*"

"*Bonsoir, Monsieur.*" In French she continued, "We have a reservation: Mitchell for four people." She had used their childhood name deliberately.

"*Bien sur.*" He and Margot chatted as he led them to a back table. It was clear Margot had been here before.

When they were all seated, Amy whispered to Margot, "What's the problem—bad food or bad service?"

Margot laughed. "We're early, by French standards. It's only 8:15. It'll fill up."

The women pondered their menus, which again had English translations. Margot said, "There are two types of fixed-price menus. One includes an appetizer, a main course, and dessert; the other includes either an appetizer and a main course, or a main course and dessert. I think I'm going to go for all three. I'm starving—and there are a couple of desserts here that are incredible!"

There was silence as they studied their menus. Margot said, "After we decide what we're having, the waitress can help us choose an appropriate wine. I hadn't realized how many French wines are never exported. It makes choosing tough sometimes, but it's also a great chance to try something completely new!"

Margot looked up and immediately a waitress came over. Margot rattled off their various choices, which the waitress memorized instead of writing anything down. Then she explained something with a smile, and Margot looked delighted.

"The maitre d' is also the owner," she explained. "He remembers me from when I brought Mom and Dad and is going to offer each of us a *kir royale* to start." At the puzzled looks, she continued,

"It's a combination of champagne and *crème de cassis*, a liqueur made from blackberries."

The waitress and Margot continued their discussion and Margot then turned to her sisters. "We're now discussing what wine to get. She is suggesting a *Chinon*, which is a very light red wine. That way it will not be too heavy for Carol's fish, but will also complement Amy's steak. Does that work for everyone?"

Carol said, "I'm leaving the decision up to you. I have no idea what to pick and I trust your judgment!"

The owner produced the *kir royales* and he and Margot had an animated conversation. Margot introduced her sisters and he smiled and shook hands with everyone.

Once they were alone, Amy said, "I could get used to this lifestyle—eating good food, drinking good wine, and being with you all."

Carol nodded. "I can't tell you how much better I feel having told you all about George. What a relief."

Sophie turned toward her. "I'm glad we can be here for you." She paused. "And for each other." She continued. "So, what's the next step for you?"

Carol said, "It's been a series of unhappy conversations for years, but my discovery of that additional credit card has created a renewed sense of urgency." She paused, started to speak, but instead pressed her lips together.

Amy reached over to squeeze her hand. "It's okay. Take your time."

Carol took a deep breath. "I've finally lost patience with George. With his anger, his irrational behaviors, his sloppy habits." Her deep sigh spoke more eloquently than words. She added quietly, "I just don't want to keep living this way." She looked scared.

Amy, as usual, was blunt in her response. "The only one who's going to work to change this situation is you. From what you've told us, George won't." She took Carol's hand and, with uncharacteristic seriousness, said, "This is hard to say, but it seems to me that, in some ways, you are enabling him. Look at it from George's point of view. He doesn't have to work, he's free to do what he wants during the day and yet still has a nice roof over his head and food to eat that's prepared for him! What reason does he have to change anything?"

Carol looked thoughtful, then blushed. "Well he'd like to get more 'action,' if you know what I mean. Believe me, the bedroom is strictly for sleeping at this point."

"Ahh, the Unmentionable Topic." Amy looked at Margot. "Can you handle this subject?"

Margot smiled and put up her hands. "Amy, I'm not thirteen anymore. And besides, this is all in the spirit of finding a solution to Carol's situation." She went on more seriously. "I agree with Amy. Look at it from George's perspective. He's got it made, or at least on every other front except that one."

Carol said, "You're right. I hadn't thought about it like that. Up to now, the biggest thing stopping me has been how upset it makes the kids when we fight."

Amy looked at her scornfully. "And your current situation is *good* for them? A father who doesn't have a job? Who's a slob and doesn't help around the house? What kind of role model is that? And all this hidden tension?"

Carol looked sad. "I know you're right. There's just never a 'good' time to have it out with him. There's enough stress going on in the kids' lives—an exam they're studying for, a big paper to write, a track meet for Brian or a volleyball game for Gwen. So I just tiptoe around, hoping not to set him off."

Amy said, "Well we can all see how well that's working." At Sophie's shocked look, Amy bristled. "It's true—it's obvious how miserable Carol is, and we now know that she's been miserable for a long time." She turned back to

Carol. "So…. what do *you* want to do? For once, don't think about everyone else. Think about Carol. What does Carol want?"

Carol sat silent for several moments. Finally she said, "As we agreed with Jean-Michel this afternoon, it isn't that simple."

Amy pushed again. "I know the final answer isn't that simple. I'm not asking for a full solution. I'm just asking that you're answer be about *you*. If you only had yourself to be concerned about, what would *you* want?"

Carol sat silent again, then looked around at all of them. "Well, I'd love to be living in a house without tension. But if that means living alone, that's scary. I've never done that and I don't know how I'd handle it." She smiled wistfully and added, "I will admit that the decrease in stress could make being a single parent *almost* worth it." She paused, then added, "And now that I think about it, the *next* best thing would be losing his messy piles of paper everywhere and his dirty laundry." She looked around at them in wonderment. "Wow, that's a big thing to say out loud."

Amy said knowingly, "Yes it is, but I'm proud of you for doing it. Saying it out loud means you've admitted to yourself that being a single parent is one option, and an appealing one on a couple of important levels. Whether you choose that course of action or not is something that is yet to be decided, but it's out there now and under consideration. I know it's not that simple, but my feeling is, how can you even start to work toward a final goal until you acknowledge what the choices are?"

Carol looked sad, relieved, and concerned all at once. "I know I feel better for saying it, but I don't know if I could ever pull it off."

Amy was cheerful. "That's okay. There's no pressure to change anything tomorrow. But you've admitted to others there is a problem, and you've also recognized the possibility of being a solo parent. You still have to figure out a realistic solution, but it's a start." She looked up as the waitress put the first courses in front of everyone. "Now let's eat!"

Many laughs and much food later, all four sat around groaning. Sophie spoke first. "Margot, why did you tell me to get that apple tart? Now I'm *so* full."

Margot responded without apology. "Because it was sinfully good, and you would be less of a person if you'd never experienced it."

Sophie laughed. "I hate to say it, but you're right. It was a necessary part of my Paris experience. And I vowed not to worry about calories this week."

Apprecié

Amy grinned. "Exactly. All the desserts were sublime. It just means that we have to keep up our mega walking regime while we're here. Somehow I think that's part of Margot's evil plan anyway."

Margot yawned. "Speaking of walking, it's time to go home to bed. And, of course, we're walking there." Lots of groans as everyone slowly rose from the table.

Amy looked around as they threaded their way to the front. "This place is packed now!" Every table was full. She glanced at her watch. "Wow, is it really 10:30?"

"Yep. Welcome to the European lifestyle."

On the walk home, Amy let Sophie and Margot take the lead and she dropped back to walk beside Carol. "Carol, there *is* one more thing I'd like you to think about, but it comes perilously close to the Evil Topic."

Carol looked apprehensive.

"You don't even have to say anything," said Amy with unusual gentleness, "but just think about it. Did you ever think you might find another man—someone other than George—attractive? Do you remember what it feels like to be in love?"

They walked in silence until Amy said, "I remember the exact day I realized I wanted Jim out of my life. And believe me, it took awhile to get there. I was terrified. Josh was only ten and I never imagined being a single mother. But now…. I would never go back to the way things were." She paused. "I've never told any of you what happened to take me to that point of no return."

Carol glanced over apprehensively. She spoke quietly. "You don't have to tell me if you don't want to."

"I know I don't, but I want to. It might help you recognize your 'moment' *when* or *if* it arrives." She took a deep breath. "You know that Jim's company had started to lose business, and I know I told all of you he was drinking pretty heavily."

Carol nodded.

Amy continued. "Well, the day he confessed to me that the company was doing badly was a very bad moment. Kind of like your first discovery of the credit card debt. I was so scared and so angry. But then…." It was obvious that she was having trouble saying what came next and Carol reached over to touch her arm gently.

Amy's breath came out as a shudder. "It had been a bad day at work—this was when I still worked for Phil, and I've told you before he was a *terrible* people manager. Some of the younger staff were really getting on my nerves and I left in the middle of the afternoon to avoid saying something I shouldn't. I thought I'd swing by and get Josh early, before his after-school program. I was thinking we could bake cookies or something. As I was driving, I got a call. It was the office, so I was sure it was one of the annoying girls to ask me some stupid question. It wasn't. It was Melinda, my best friend. And she sounded awful. She said the hospital had just called and Jim and Josh had been in a car accident. She told me neither was seriously hurt, but that I needed to go right over there."

"Honestly, Carol, I don't remember that drive at all. I ran into the emergency room and was taken right back to the cubical where Josh was lying on the emergency room gurney. He was all alone, and there was blood all over his t-shirt. He looked scared, and had obviously been crying. He had a big gauze bandage on one side of his head and he cried out as soon as he saw me. I just crushed him in a hug and he started to cry again. He told me, through his sobs, that they had been in an intersection and someone had hit Jim's side of the car. Josh said he had hit his head on the door when the car had been pushed sideways." Amy looked unseeingly at Carol, obviously haunted by the images in her head as she re-lived those moments. "I never wanted to let him go, but I knew I needed to find Jim. He was unconscious and as soon as I saw him I could smell the alcohol. He had a concussion, but otherwise was fine."

"It turned out that Jim had lost another contract and gone out drinking with some of his work buddies. Apparently he decided it was a good idea to go get Josh to have some father/son bonding time and he thought he was 'fine' to drive."

"Later I talked to the policeman who was first on the scene. He told me that Jim had run a red light. Thank God the passengers in the other car were okay and they didn't sue! But both cars had been badly damaged."

Amy turned to Carol and there were tears on her cheeks. "Seeing Josh like that was the worst experience of my life. The next day I went to a lawyer and started divorce proceedings."

Carol was silent for a moment. "Wow," she said under her breath.

Amy looked over, saying, "George is putting your family in danger, too. And you now know you can't trust him. I wanted you to know that I understand from my own personal experience how scared you are. And how hard this is. Any time that you need someone to talk to, please call me, okay?"

Carol nodded. They looked at each other a moment, then hurried to catch up with Margot and Sophie.

Arriving back at the apartment, everyone quickly readied for bed and turned in. Margot spoke to Sophie's and Amy's backs as they headed to the smaller bedroom. "No alarm clocks here. We'll get up when we wake up, and take it from there."

Amy sighed. "My kind of place. Goodnight."

Amid a chorus of goodnights, Margot turned off the lights and silence settled in.

Chapter 16. Sophie

Sophie woke slowly. The light on her eyelids was muted and soft, not the bright light she was used to. After a quick moment, her mind told her what her body already knew: she was in Paris, not in Salt Lake, and the light was muted because it was filtering in through the wooden shades that covered the window. Looking over, she could see that Amy was still asleep. Moving quietly, Sophie squeezed between the beds and went out into the living room. Hearing a noise in the kitchen, she peeked around the corner. "Good morning."

Margot turned and smiled. "Good morning. How'd you sleep?"

"Great. I was worried I would have problems after eating all that food so late, but I slept like a log."

"Good. Me too. I find I often wake up a couple of times the first night here, but I go right back to sleep. Looks like we have enough milk for lattes, so I'm off to the bakery. Want anything in particular?"

"How about a croissant?"

"Those are already on my list. And I was thinking of getting a *pain au chocolat* for Amy, the chocolate nut."

"That's a good idea. Have you taken your shower?"

"Yep. Go ahead. Carol wasn't moving yet, and I'm assuming Amy isn't?"

Sophie shook her head and headed toward the bathroom. She heard Margot quietly close the outside door. As the hot water poured over her head, she let her thoughts go back to Roger and the discussion they'd had about this trip....

****

Sophie was on the computer, looking up the dates and comparing her trip to the school calendar, when Roger walked past. Their computer sat in an alcove just off the bedroom, with a small window looking over the back yard. Looking up, she realized this was probably her best chance to discuss the trip with him.

"Roger, do you have a minute?"

He stopped and turned. "Sure, what's up?"

"I spoke to Margot today."

"Great. How's she doing? This thing with your mom has been hard on all of you."

"You're right. She's doing okay, but that's part of what we were talking about. We were talking about Mom, and the weekend chemo schedule, and how much better she's doing now. That led to a discussion about how long it's been since we've all been together. Margot is suggesting that all four sisters meet for a long weekend."

Roger nodded. "Sounds logical. Tough for you with your travel schedule, though."

Sophie nodded. "I was just checking that. It looks like I could get away for five days in late May. The kids' schedules start clearing out by then as well. There will be one last soccer game for Jeremy, and Bobby's tennis schedule will be done by then."

"Five days seems like a long time. Where are you thinking about going? Florida? Las Vegas to see your parents? Seems like you could take less time. Why not go on a Friday and be back Sunday night?"

"Actually, Margot has invited us to Paris to their apartment. Remember they bought a place there three or four years ago? To go that far, we figure we need five days, since two of those are travel days."

There was silence. She looked up from the computer to see Roger's face set in cold lines of anger.

"What?" She was shocked.

He didn't say anything for a moment, then mumbled, "Nothing."

It was obvious that there was something. She stood up and went over to him, putting her hand on his arm. "What is it?"

He shrugged off her hand. "It just seems like a long time for you to be away, and a long way to go. Do you really need to go to Paris, of all places?"

She nodded. "Everyone else seems to be excited about the idea. I admit, I was too, until your reaction. None of us has been there except Margot, so it feels like an adventure."

Roger's look didn't change. "You're already away so much for work that another five days for a 'girls' weekend' seems excessive. I guess I just thought you'd want to be with us—me and the boys—during the little vacation time you have."

Sophie was incredulous. "So this is something personal? That I'm choosing to spend time with my sisters instead of you guys? That's not it at all. Roger, my sisters and I haven't spent any time together for years. We were very close growing up, and this thing with Mom has made us realize that we've lost something that was very special. We want to see if we can find that closeness again."

Roger stayed silent for a moment before speaking quietly. "I thought *we* were your family now."

Tears came into Sophie's eyes, to her own surprise. "Of course you're my family, but that doesn't mean that my old family ceases to exist. It might have seemed that way to you, I can understand that because I haven't seen them much in recent years, but we want to fix that. It doesn't mean that I feel any differently about you or the boys. It's not a case of either/or. You can love more than three people."

Roger said, "We already don't see you as much as we'd like, with your working and traveling and the evening commitments even when you're home."

Sophie had been so excited while looking at flight reservations, but now she felt deflated. Was he right? How could she be thinking of a trip so far away, without her family? All of her ongoing guilty feelings about not spending enough time with the kids surfaced with a vengeance. And somehow it stung more when *he* was playing the 'guilty' card than when she played it on herself.

Roger seemed to be reading her mind with his next words. "I don't feel like the kids see you enough as it is, and now you're saying you want to leave us for yet another commitment."

Roger's words erased the guilt and replaced it with anger. How *dare* he? She provided for this family and that meant she sometimes had to sacrifice being with them. She didn't enjoy it—it was just a part of being the sole provider. Her business trips were often lonely and dull, and always exhausting.

Stepping back, she could understand his position, but reconnecting with her sisters was a much more important commitment than any work-related one. She would not give up on this trip before it had even begun.

"I'm sorry you feel that way, Roger. I didn't know how much my travel and evening schedule bothered you. I'll be happy to try to work to change both of those things, but please don't ask me to give up this chance to reconnect with my sisters. I know that they have not been a big part of my life for the last few years, but that's not an indication of how important they are to me."

Roger looked away, then looked back at her. "How important am I to you?"

Sophie was stunned. "You are *very* important to me. How can you even ask that?" She felt her stomach drop. What kind of question was that? This was sounding like there was more of an issue here than just this proposed trip.

"It doesn't feel that way recently, and this feels like another string to pull you away."

Sophie took his hand and, in doing so, realized that the physical touch felt strange. How long had it been since she had held his hand? Had she been too engrossed in work to notice that she and Roger weren't talking and doing things together anymore? She couldn't remember the last time the two of them had done anything without the kids along. "Roger, you're right. We've both been busy lately, you with kid stuff and me with work stuff. Let's go out to dinner Friday night, just the two of us, maybe see a movie?"

Roger took his hand away. "Friday is a booster club meeting."

"Okay, how about Saturday night?"

"Jeremy and I will be away for a soccer tournament."

"Okay, will you be back in time for Sunday brunch?"

Roger smiled, but the smile didn't seem to reach his eyes. "Probably."

Sophie smiled back. "Great!" she exclaimed, pretending everything was fine. "Roger, this trip with my sisters is very important to me. Please understand that."

His smile instantly faded. "I'm trying to understand, but it still feels like one more thing taking you away from us."

Sophie sighed. "I'm sorry you feel that way." Her voice strengthened. "But this is something I need to do. For myself, for Mom, for my sisters."

Roger didn't answer, but instead walked out of the room. Sophie sat down on the bed, feeling defiant. The conversation had only made her more certain that this trip was an important step for her and her sisters. She got up slowly and went back to the computer, where the flight schedule was blinking. Sitting down, she finished making her reservation and hit Enter. It was done.

So why didn't she feel happier?

****

There was a thud on the door.

"Hey, stop hogging the shower. My turn!" came Amy's indignant voice.

"Fine, fine," laughed Sophie. She wrapped up in a heated towel and pulled open the door. "All yours."

Half an hour later they sat down to home-brewed lattes, a fresh baguette cut into long strips, warm croissants, and sweet butter, honey, jam, and yogurt. While the others started eating enthusiastically, Margot said, "Two of us need to go up the street to order our rotisserie chicken from the butcher for our dinner tonight, plus go to the cheese store, and then to the grocery for *Coca Light* and paper products, stuff like that. The other two can go to the open-air market that is along the way and pick up whatever looks good to have with our chicken tonight. We also need snacks for the next several days. Does that sound reasonable?"

"But we don't all speak French," protested Amy.

"I know but, to be honest, they're going to try to speak English with you anyway—and pointing works, too."

Carol laughed. "I'm willing to give it a try. Amy, why don't you come with me to the market and we'll see what we can find?"

Amy agreed, but was surprised by Carol's reaction. Was this really her cautious and nervous sister? "Okay, as long as you do the talking and use the hand gestures. You seem more comfortable with the money already."

Margot turned to Sophie. "That means you're with me."

"That sounds good. I need to pick up some tampons anyway."

Margot said, "I try to keep some handy here, but I think I'm out at the moment. Bad timing, huh?"

Sophie made a face. "At this point, it's becoming on again/off again, so I think I'm about done with it. Thank God!"

Margot grimaced. "Not me. Still every 30 days, like clockwork. Oh well, maybe when I'm old like you!"

"Watch it, sister. You aren't that far behind me. Your time is coming sooner than you think."

"To be honest, I'm ready," Margot admitted. "I've had my two kids. Who needs the hassle?"

All four women nodded in agreement.

"Speaking of kids," said Amy, "I did hear from Josh yesterday, and so far the house is still standing and he hasn't broken any bones. I have to say I *love* texting—it lets me feel like I know what's going on with Josh in a way that's not possible otherwise. And now I have a whole new reason to love it—I can keep in touch with him from very far away, and it doesn't cost me a fortune."

"I used to think it was dumb," said Carol as she buttered her bread. "I mean, why wouldn't you just call someone? But then I had teenagers and now I understand."

"Don't you just love how 'stealth' it is?" Amy spoke as she reached into the basket. "You can send a message, saying, 'Where the hell are you?' and they can respond without looking 'uncool' to their friends. Nobody knows it's their Mom on the other end of the conversation." She bit into a croissant and her eyes widened.

"Wow, this one's got chocolate inside!"

Margot laughed. "That's a *pain au chocolat*. Seemed your style."

"Absolutely!"

Carol held up the honey jar. "This is really good too. Where's it from?"

"That's from Vezelay, about two hours south of here. We were down there for a weekend trip and the woman selling it said that it was collected when the sunflowers were in bloom, so it's mostly sunflower pollen. That's why it's so yellow."

"Incredible!" Carol added more to her bread. "Can we buy some here?"

"Not that particular kind, but there is a local beekeeper at the market. Keep an eye out for his honey when you're walking around."

"Will do." Carol asked, "Anything in particular you want, or are you leaving it up to us?"

"I'd like an avocado or two for our salad. I don't how they get such good ones this early in the year—I think they must come from southern Europe or North Africa. And I'd love some fresh flowers. There's a stand at the far end of the market. Choose some good veggies, too. When you're walking around you'll see what's in season."

After all the dishes were done, Margot pulled out a canvas bag with two small wheels on one end, and two French net sacks. "Amy, the sacks are for you and Carol. You'll be surprised how much they hold. Sophie and I will take the canvas bag since we're buying wine and soda."

All four set off through the first door, across the courtyard, out the second door to the street, and then up the block. Rounding the corner, they could see that the open space along the middle of the large street was now filled with three colorful rows of covered stalls. Loud voices were hawking various products.

Amy spoke first. "*So* cool! Fruit, vegetables, meat, eggs, flowers, clothing.... Man, you can get a little of everything here!"

Margot smiled. "Enjoy! We'll meet you back here in half an hour."

Margot and Sophie continued up the street while Amy and Carol started down the first row. Margot knew the vendors had spotted Amy when she heard various voices saying "Good Morning!" in heavily accented English behind her. Margot laughed and said, "They'll do just fine."

Sophie nodded. "You're right, but I admit I'm glad to be with you. I'm not quite ready to be on my own yet."

Margot looked at Sophie as she answered, "You'd be fine, but I'm glad to have *you* with *me*." They maneuvered through the crowded market and came out the other side. "That's the butcher up there," Margot pointed up the hill. "The supermarket and *fromagerie* are just beyond it. Luckily, it's downhill on the way home!"

Margot stopped at the butcher and arranged to pick up their cooked chicken at 7:30. As they turned into the supermarket, she warned Sophie, "This is much smaller than the supermarkets at home, but it's got the basics."

They walked up and down the aisles, collecting soda, wine, crackers and snacks in the rolling bag. Margot said, "I know that when the bag's full, that's all I can manage to get home!"

Margot moved with confidence through the aisles, but Sophie found herself getting distracted by the novelty all around her. Some things looked the same, or at least similar, to home, but then she'd come to a section that was completely new. The canned food aisle, for instance. There were all kinds of things that looked completely different and she kept losing Margot as she stopped to read labels. When it was time to check out, Margot found

Sophie, totally engrossed, at the yogurt section. "There must be twenty different kinds of yogurt," said Sophie in amazement. "And some things look like yogurt, but are called other things—what's *fromage blanc*?"

"It's made from cow's milk that's been drained. It's a little thicker than yogurt, more like cottage cheese or cream cheese, but with fewer calories. I love it with a little sugar for a healthy dessert."

Sophie nodded. "Can we get some? I'd like to try it." She noticed Margot's bag was full. "Oh, sorry, you ready to go? I keep finding things to look at."

They moved quickly through the checkout line and across the street to the *fromagerie*.

Wonderful sights and smells assailed Sophie when she stepped into the shop. The glass display case that ran the length of the shop was filled with a variety of cheeses—from small, round, goat cheeses, which ranged from pure white to dark gray, to large blocks of Swiss *Emmenthal*. The air was filled with their sharp tang and with the sweet smell of honey from an open jar on the counter. Sophie could also smell fresh butter, and Margot pointed out the large block of it behind the display case, which the saleswoman was cutting into chunks to sell. Soon they had several small, wrapped packages that went on top of the items already in the bag. Sophie wrinkled her nose.

"Margot, that last cheese smells like it's rotten. Do you really like it?"

Margot nodded and said, "That's *Epoisse*. I discovered that one when Paul and I went to Burgundy where they produce it. I know it smells stinky, but it's really incredible spread on a fresh baguette. I really think you'll like it—especially when you combine it with a nice glass of red wine from the same region."

Once outside, Margot pulled Sophie out of the flow of people and turned to her.

"Sophie, you seem quiet this morning. More than just because you don't speak French. Is anything wrong?"

Sophie was silent for a moment. "Actually, I've been thinking about Roger."

Margot looked over to check Sophie's expression. "Did he give you a hard time about coming?"

Sophie nodded. "Yeah. At first he seemed okay with the idea of a 'girls' weekend,' but when I told him it would be five days and in Paris, suddenly he wasn't so happy anymore." She was silent, then continued. "He saw it as another thing pulling me away, and took it as a personal affront. I know it's hard on them because I travel so much, but this is different and I thought he would understand that."

Sophie was silent for another moment then said, "When I said it was about re-connecting to family, he said that he thought he and the boys were my family now." She turned to Margot. "Both his parents are dead, and his one brother lives in Alaska—so I do understand that the boys and I play that part for him. But I was surprised he was so unsympathetic to my wanting to reconnect with you guys."

Margot looked thoughtful. "Maybe he sees it as a threat. Maybe he's afraid that this will somehow take something away from him—not just now, but in the future. I hoped he would look at it as a chance to have more family around, maybe making up for the fact that he doesn't have much of his own."

Sophie nodded. "That's what I was hoping, too, but apparently he felt the opposite!" She sighed. "Things are not great right now between us."

Margot searched Sophie's face for clues. "How so?"

"Well, I realized when we had the disagreement about my coming here that we haven't had much to say to each other for a while now. And anything physical—well, that's not happening either. I don't know. I figured it was just that I was busy with work, and he was busy with the kids' schedules, but all of a sudden I realized we had not really talked in forever. I suggested dinner and it took three tries to come up with a time we could get together. We finally fit in a brunch on Sunday, and I tried reaching out to him, but he was still hurt about the trip."

Margot nodded. "Having teenagers is really stressful. At least that's what I'm finding. Is that the problem?"

Sophie said, "I honestly don't know. It definitely seems like we've drifted apart. I think that's one of the reasons I'm so tense at home."

"Well, you are awfully busy. What if you tried rearranging your schedule when you get back?"

Sophie did not look convinced. "I've already promised that, but to be honest, I'm not sure it will be that easy. I can work on the obvious things, like attending fewer events in the evenings, stuff like that, and the boys' schedules are much less hectic in the summer." She paused and looked very sad suddenly. Margot reached over and squeezed her shoulder.

"What? Is there something else?"

Sophie nodded and her eyes filled with tears. This frightened Margot more than anything else could have. This was her big, strong, unbeatable sister. What could possibly bring Sophie to her knees?

Sophie took a deep breath, which she let out very slowly, trying to get a grip. "I think.... I think he's having an affair."

Margot was stunned. "Wow, that's quite a big step from not having dinner together."

"I know. Something happened recently." Margot waited for her to go on, and after taking a couple of moments to get her composure back, Sophie began to speak again. "It was about two o'clock and I had just left a meeting with a company whose offices are near our house. I remembered a book I'd meant to take that morning to lend to a friend at work. When I got home, I expected Roger to be there, but the house was quiet. Okay, so I figured he was out running errands. I went up and found the book, then got back in my car. I called him, figuring I'd just say hello, and... I just said that I was between meetings and wanted to say hello." She paused and looked up at Margot. "You know what he said? He said he was at home watching a basketball game." She paused again. "I didn't know what to say. How could I then tell him, 'No you're not; I have just left there'? So I talked for another minute about dinner or something, honestly I don't even remember, then hung up and just sat there. Why would he lie about that?"

Margot shook her head, trying to think of a benign reason.

"If he was running errands, you'd think he would have said that. He didn't need to say he was home."

"Could you hear anything in the background?"

"I don't think so. I was so flustered that I just wanted to get off the phone."

Margot chose her words carefully. "Well, it's weird, I agree, but it doesn't necessarily mean something bad. Maybe he was getting you something?"

"I don't think so. That was two weeks ago and he hasn't said anything since."

"Maybe he had a doctor's appointment and didn't want to scare you?"

Sophie looked skeptical. "I can't think of anything he would need to hide. I'm now keeping a closer eye out for other possible evidence. Nothing yet, but it's driving me a little crazy."

"Do you think you should talk to him about it?"

"At first I didn't want to, but it's eating at me. I think I'm going to have to."

Margot paused. "Do you want to talk about it over dinner with Carol and Amy? They might have some good ideas."

Sophie shook her head slightly. "Not tonight. I'm not quite ready to admit it out loud to more than one person. But maybe before the weekend is through. It would be nice to hear some other logical explanations that I haven't thought of."

"Exactly. Okay, I won't say anything, but I do think it would be a good idea to talk it through. It won't go any further; you know that."

Sophie smiled fully for the first time. "I do know. I love you, little sister."

How long had it been since they'd said those words to each other? Margot hugged Sophie. "I love you too. It's funny how easy it is to fall into some of our old patterns now that we're all together again, but it also feels different." Margot smiled warmly. "It was always you taking care of the rest of us. Now maybe we can return the favor."

For a long moment, they shared a look full of understanding. Then Margot glanced down at her watch. "Yikes, we only have a few minutes 'til we're late, and you know Carol will start worrying if she doesn't see us within two minutes of the appointed time."

Sophie laughed. "True, true. Okay, let's go." She laid her hand on Margot's arm. "Thanks for listening."

Margot squeezed her hand wordlessly.

Five minutes later, they rounded the corner and saw Carol and Amy in the marketplace. "So much for not standing out!" said Margot, laughing. Amy was deep in conversation with a vendor of teapots.

"What's going on?" asked Margot. "I thought you didn't speak French."

Amy laughed. "I don't, but it turns out I don't need to. He's been trying to sell me this blue teapot and pick me up at the same time, all in very broken English." She smiled at the young man behind the table and said, "See? Here are my friends!" He smiled at them all and said, with a heavy French accent, "Fifteen euros? It is very cheap." His smile was charming.

"Oh, alright!" Amy pulled a twenty-euro bill from her pocket and he wrapped the pot in some newspaper before putting it into a bag and handing it to her.

"And maybe we see each other later?"

Amy smiled back. "No, no, I'm sorry. But *merci* for the beautiful teapot."

He looked regretful, but not surprised, and bowed as they left the stall.

As they walked back to the apartment, Margot asked, "How did you guys do? From the size of those bags, you had some success."

"Did we ever!" Carol grinned. "Everything is so fresh and everyone's so nice. We got all kinds of salad stuff, and fresh beans, and artichokes, and look at these flowers.... I didn't realize you could have such a great variety of food in a street market. Is it always like this?"

"Yeah, isn't that amazing? We have a good weekly farmers' market at home, but it doesn't have nearly as many things as these do here. This same group sets up at different locations in Paris every day."

"Wow, even in winter?"

"I'm not sure. I haven't been here in January or February, but I know it's here in the fall."

Margot continued to speak as they went through the courtyard. "Sophie and I ordered the chicken and bought several different kinds of cheese, from very stinky to very mild. I hope you'll try them all!"

Amy sighed. "More wonderful food! Okay, so we drop all this stuff off. Then what?"

"Then we'll head to the bus and go over to the Latin Quarter. I figured we'd walk around there, do a little shopping, go see the tapestries if we have time and the inclination, and then come home to our scrumptious meal. We need to pick up the chicken at 7:30."

After a quick emptying of the various bags onto counters and into the refrigerator, everyone gathered cameras, maps, and umbrellas and headed out the door once again to follow Margot to the bus stop. Sophie said nothing about her revelation, which was weighing heavily on Margot's heart. Was there any good reason for a married man to lie about being home when he wasn't? What might he be doing right now, with Sophie out of the country? Surely Sophie was wondering the same things....

Chapter 17. Amy

Amy was glad Margot had suggested they take the bus instead of the metro to the Left Bank and the Latin Quarter area. There was so much to see along the way that they would have missed underground. The buildings were fascinating. Margot had said that many were built in the late 1800s, but each had its own personality. Some had beautiful ironwork on the balconies; some had overflowing flowerpots hanging everywhere, and some looked like they were in need of some good old-fashioned TLC. Margot pointed out the street that led back to the Place des Vosges and Amy thought Carol craned her neck for a look into the square. The buildings as they got closer to the river were even older, dating from the 1600s and 1700s. Many of them were plain white, without balconies, but their arched doorways gave intriguing glimpses of greenery and interesting courtyards inside. The bus drove down a wide, busy street, then turned to cross a bridge.

"This is where lots of the city's offices are," Margot said. "And see, just on the other side of these buildings—there's Notre Dame! We'll come back by there on our way home." They rode across another bridge and, just on the other side, Margot guided them off the bus.

"This is where I spent most of my time when I was a student at the Sorbonne." She smiled. "That's when my love for Paris began, and it's never faded."

Amy grinned and looked around. "I can see why. Cafés on every corner, lots of shops, and cute men—some are kinda short, though." Everyone laughed.

Margot shepherded them up a narrow street. "There are lots of small shops along here to look at. We'll follow this up to Boulevard St. Germain, one of the main streets of the Latin Quarter."

Amy fell into step next to Margot, leaving Carol and Sophie to walk behind them. Amy said, "This is really a great trip already. Thanks again for inviting us. It wasn't an easy decision for the rest of us, but it's obvious now what a good idea it was."

Margot said, "It's made me realize that, like Carol, I don't have anyone to talk to at home about all these kinds of issues." Silently she was thinking about Sophie and she hoped that Sophie would also open herself up to their advice and support.

"Me neither." Amy reached over to squeeze Margot's hand. "Let's keep this going after we get back." Amy's expression changed as she gazed across the street. "Ooh, look at that store."

They all stopped. "This place has great posters and cards," said Margot. "The two framed posters hanging in the living room are from here."

"Let's go in, then!" Amy was already crossing the threshold. Twenty minutes later, everyone walked out with rolled bundles under their arms.

Unlike shopping at home, which was always hurried and purposeful, this expedition was spontaneous. Amy especially loved how they just stopped in any store they wanted. No destination, but lots of stops. There was a randomness to it that appealed to her sense of destiny. In the window of a men's store, she saw a shirt that immediately reminded her of Josh, and she went in to buy it for him.

A couple of hours later, Margot directed them to a small Italian restaurant off the main street. As soon as they walked in, the noise and bustle outside receded. A handsome man with dark, slicked-back hair approached them. *"Bonjour,*

Mesdames." His eyes swept over the four of them. *"Vous dejeunez?"*

Margot answered. *"Oui,* we are here for lunch."

They all sat down at a small table overlooking the street, gratefully piling their various packages in one corner.

Margot said, "When the weather is nice like this, you get everyone coming out to walk around, even if it's just during their lunch break." She added, "The pizza is very good here, though you'll see it's a little different from home. Some of the ingredients are rather unexpected."

They were quiet as they all looked over their menus.

Amy broke the silence. "Like this one with the cooked egg on top? Why not? And with capers and olives, please." She looked over at Margot.

"Good choice." Everyone else chimed in with requests and Margot quickly placed the order. The waiter returned almost immediately with their drinks. He lingered next to Amy after setting her beer down.

"You are American?" he asked her in heavily-accented English.

Amy nodded.

"I speak little English. I practice?" He asked this with a gentle smile and a long look into her eyes.

Amy laughed. "Sure. Practice."

He smiled back. "Where you are from?"

"Las Vegas."

His look was one of astonishment. "You live there? The place for gambling?"

She nodded. "Yep. People live there, too."

He nodded enthusiastically. "I want to go there one day. When I have money. I come visit you?"

She laughed again. "Well, maybe!"

He looked crestfallen. "You not think I am good man?"

Amy said, "I'm sure you are a nice man. I just don't know you."

He smiled again and put out his hand. "Jacques is my name. *Enchantez.*"

She shook his hand. "Amy." She gestured around the table. "And these are my sisters, Sophie, Margot, and Carol."

He smiled at each woman, but then someone from the kitchen shouted something in an annoyed voice and he hurried away.

Amy looked around at her sisters. "Looks like lots of the natives are friendly."

Carol agreed. "My turn yesterday; your turn today."

Sophie added, "That's *two* in one day for Amy—and it's only lunchtime!"

"I can't help it if I seem to be in demand around here," Amy said with mock innocence.

Margot said, "You must know you have that look that attracts attention. Sophie, you have it too."

Sophie looked amazed. "I see it in Amy, but I certainly don't see it in myself."

"I disagree. Amy may have more of it, but you've got it too. It's a warmth, a vitality, that makes men turn their heads." Margot paused. "I admit I've always been envious of that."

It was now Amy's turn to look astonished. "*You* envious of *us*? You, Ms. Perfect Size 8?"

Margot said, "Size-wise, I guess I'm okay, but I definitely don't have that extra something. I'd forgotten about it until this trip. Growing up, I would feel like I was doing pretty well in one social situation or another, and then one of you would show up and suddenly the attention was no longer on whatever I was talking about."

Amy exclaimed, "I never knew that! I always felt envious of you that you seemed able to stay slim without trying too hard. I was always fighting the extra pounds."

"Well, when I was in high school, I didn't have to work at being slim, but I definitely do now—and it gets harder each year. Plus at home it's so hard to find the time to do any exercise. That's one of the things I like about being here. I always loved to walk, and here, it's such fun and so interesting that it doesn't feel like exercise!"

"I will agree with that." Amy was stopped from continuing by the arrival of the pizzas.

"Wow," said Carol, breathing deeply. "That smells incredible."

Sophie spoke up. "He brought us a basket of bread, too. Why's that?"

Margot answered, "They always do."

"But with pizza?"

"I know, but bread is part of every meal. You take a piece and put it next to your plate."

"That's another thing I've noticed," said Carol. "Everyone puts it on the table, not on their plate. And there is no butter and no bread plate."

"True. They seem to feel that the table is a perfectly fine place for bread. You don't have to eat any if you don't want to."

"I know, but I have to admit that it will come in handy when sopping up this amazing sauce!"

As everyone finished, the waiter came back and took orders for coffee, again spending extra time trying to talk to Amy. After he left, Amy looked around at all of them and spoke. "So, since we are making confessions, I have to tell you that I am envious of all of your lives that seem to be so together. I feel like I should have my act together. I'm 47, yet I'm still always one step away from bankruptcy. How can I get myself on that success track that you all seem to have found?"

Carol spoke first. "Slow down and let's talk about that for a minute. At work things are going well for me, but as you heard, the home front is not so pretty. I think people always have hidden problems. You certainly shouldn't envy me!"

Margot nodded. "Appearances can be deceiving."

Amy looked at Margot. "But look at you. A successful job, enough money to buy a place in Paris, two gorgeous boys, a wonderful husband...."

Margot was silent for a moment before saying quietly, "That's how it looks, anyway." She paused again and everyone could see she was thinking through what she was going to say. Clearing her throat, she said, "Okay. Shall we talk about me for a second? Yes, I am in a good job that makes good money, and that's why we could buy the apartment. But what you don't know is that we got word last week that the company is being sold, and depending on who buys it, I could be unemployed in two months."

Everyone was silent, taking this news in. "Yikes," breathed Amy. "That's a bummer."

Margot laughed weakly. "You could say that."

"Do you think you'll lose your job?"

"Probably. The most likely buyer for the company has set certain terms already."

"I have to admit that I really don't understand what exactly you do," said Carol. "Can you explain it?"

"Sure. I basically act as a middleman—or middle-woman—between people who want to lease office space, and people who have space to lease. In past jobs, I always leased space for outside owners. In this job, which I got two years ago, I'm working for a company that owns office buildings across the country, so the leasing is internal. That's a big advantage because it means I can't be 'fired' for some random reason. I just work with my staff to set the budget at the beginning of each year, and then all year we fill any vacant space. Does that make sense?"

"I have to say it's the first time I've understood what you do," said Amy. "You are definitely doing something most people just don't think about on a day-to-day basis."

"True. I sometimes think of it as a 'stealth' occupation. If you say 'real estate' people always think of home sales, never office leases."

"So what will you do if you get laid off?" asked Carol, looking worried.

"I'm not sure yet. I could go back to my old company, but a lot of people that I knew there have left, so I don't think that's a good choice. With all the various mergers in my field, there are fewer companies to choose from."

Sophie spoke up for the first time. "Well, the good news is, you have twenty years of experience. You'll find something."

Margot looked tense. "There are some very talented, very aggressive young women right behind me, and that's scary."

"Are you guys okay for money if you have some down time?" asked Carol.

"For a couple of months, yes. We have some money in a fund we earmarked for college. That is obviously what we hope it will be used for, but if we end up needing to use some of that money now, so be it. I really hope we won't have to dig into it, but it's there if we need it."

"Well, that's good. Plus you bought your house a long time ago. Is it almost paid off?"

Margot nodded. "We've refinanced a couple of times to add on to the house, but the mortgage isn't too bad. I'm more worried about the apartment. We only bought it three years ago, and we owe much more on it than we owe on our home."

Amy looked worried. "Good point. Man, I hope you won't have to sell it. How's the market over here?"

"Actually very good, so we could sell it." Margot paused. "But I won't do that unless we absolutely have to. Paul and I talk about our future trips here all the time. It's part of our dreams for the future." She was silent.

Carol spoke up quietly. "Please let us know what we can do to help. We can all give moral support, if nothing else."

Margot sighed. "Thanks. Hopefully that'll be all I need." She looked up and made an obvious effort to smile. "Enough morbid talk. Let's get back out there and do some more shopping!"

Amy laughed. "Funny how spending money can always cheer a girl up. Okay, let's go."

Margot got the attention of the waiter to bring the check, then turned back to Amy. "You're going to have to say goodbye to your boyfriend."

Amy sighed, doing her best to look worn out by the attention. "You know, it's always this way for us celebrities." Everyone laughed. Even the waiter changed his frown to a smile seeing them all laughing.

"You will come back to visit me?" he asked hopefully, giving his best soulful look at Amy.

"I will try, my friend, but I must go where my sisters lead."

He took a page from his order book and wrote quickly. "Here is my name and my number."

Amy took it, then shook his hand. "You are very sweet, but believe me, you do not know how much trouble I would be."

He said earnestly, "I take care of you."

She smiled. "I am sure you would try."

All four women gathered their belongings and said, "*Merci. Au revoir, Monsieur.*"

"*Au revoir, Mesdames.*" He followed them to the door and waved as they started walking up the street. Amy turned back to wave, then turned to Carol.

"So you and I both have someone to come back to! Think we can find guys for Sophie and Margot? Tougher job, right?"

Carol laughed. "Ah well, there is someone for everyone. We'll do our best, but they may have to find their own guys."

Margot and Sophie both managed to look affronted for a moment, then broke into laughter. "I just want to find a good pair of black sandals," said Margot.

Margot and Sophie linked arms, and Carol and Amy followed behind, all four laughing and getting more attention than they realized.

Amy felt a wave of happiness flow through her. The attention she'd gotten from both men made her feel attractive and alive. The daily cares of life and work could be left on the back burner for the day. They'd be right there when she was ready to deal with them, but in the meantime she was out to have fun. She knew she did want advice, and listening to Margot and Carol's stories made bringing up her own issues about work and Andrew easier. Carol was right—you never knew what was going on in people's lives. Her sisters' 'perfect' lives weren't so perfect. They'd be good sounding boards for her when the time was right....

Chapter 18. Margot

Four hours later, and with several more packages each, we stumbled onto the bus and headed home. Back at the apartment, we dumped our bags and slumped onto the couch and chairs in the living room.

"Phew!" said Amy. "Talk about power shopping!"

I looked around. "Why don't we all take a break, and then at 7:00 or so someone can make the salad and cook veggies while I'm getting the chicken? How does that sound?"

Carol spoke up first. "I never take naps at home, but that's where I'm headed. Is there an alarm to wake us up? I'm afraid if I lie down I won't get back up!"

"I don't think I'm going to sleep," I said. "I'm going to get on the computer and see what's new at work. I'll get everybody up."

Soon everyone settled in and it was quiet. I made myself a cup of coffee and took it out to the table in the living room, where I pulled out the laptop to check e-mail. I answered a few that seemed the most pressing, then found an announcement that one of my partners had forwarded. It was an update on the status of the sale of the company. It looked like Vector Associates was going to buy us, and if that happened, I would be unemployed. Vector outsourced everything and wouldn't be keeping on any personnel.

I sat back in my chair, letting the reality of being unemployed sink in. Okay, so as of August first I would be out of a job. That meant I really needed to start thinking about options. I knew I didn't want to go back to my old company. The more I thought about it, the more I saw only two choices for me. The first would be to wait to see who ended up getting Vector's business and going to work for them, since I had experience with the properties that they were buying. The second choice would be to decide if there was anyone I'd want to partner with at one of the remaining companies. That would mean effectively starting over. It would take time to build my client base again.

Looking at the email, I felt both sadness and regret. The move to this company two years ago had been everything I'd hoped for. I was working with great people and doing what I wanted to do. We had all often commented on how much fun it was and what a good team we had. It had seemed too good to be true — and now it turned out it was.

Maybe I could take a little time off before starting the new job, whatever it would be. Come back to Paris and just de-stress for a while.

No, realistically, that wasn't going to happen. There would be too much pressure to get another job because I knew one thing for sure: I was determined not to have to sell this apartment.

I looked up to find Amy standing in front of me.

"Wow, you were miles away."

"Sorry about that. What time is it?"

"Just about 7:15, Mrs. Alarm Clock. Want to walk over to get the chicken?"

"Sounds good. Sorry about that. I completely lost track of time."

"No problem. I'll go tell Sophie and Carol that it's time to start waking up."

I closed the computer, and grabbed money and keys.

We walked for a block in silence before Amy spoke.

"So where were you back there? An e-mail send you off?"

I sighed. "I just got confirmation that my company is being sold to Vector Associates, so I'll probably be out of a job as of August first. It seems unbelievable, even as I say it out loud to you."

"I'm sorry to hear it." Amy squeezed my shoulder. "Are you totally freaked out?"

"No. It's not real to me yet. I'll probably try for a job with whomever they give the business to, since I've been working on the properties for two years now. The problem is that the competition for that business will be fierce. There are a lot of people who would love to have that client and those properties. " I started to feel angry. "You know what the worst thing is? We had put together such a great team. That's what will be the hardest to find again."

"It is amazing how incredibly important the people you work with are," agreed Amy. "You spend so much of your day with them. Not to mention you need to be able to trust them."

"I totally agree." I turned to look at her. "Your new company is doing okay, right? You and Melinda were smart to start your own shop. I'm very proud of you for taking that jump, you know. You were saying earlier today that you don't feel like a success, but I disagree. None of the rest of us has formed our own company—and done it successfully, I might add."

Amy looked worried. "It's been successful so far, but this new guy we took on as a partner is worrying me. I was just telling Melinda before I left that I have a bad feeling about him. Nothing too specific, but he just seems too confident about things that are not certainties. He's a big schmoozer, which is just what we wanted—someone to help us grow the business. But I'm starting to wonder if there is anything beyond the hot air. I was reviewing his expense reports before I left, and he knows how to spend money, that much is for sure. Whether he is actually getting any new business, I don't know."

"You have to spend money to make money, so hopefully that's what he's doing. Why do you doubt him?"

"Partly instinct, I guess. Something is not adding up right. I figure we'll have a conversation when I get back, to bring me up to speed on his progress, and just get him to tell me who he's been meeting with. I've been in the business long enough to know if he's talking to the right people."

"Sounds like a reasonable approach. That way, if he's legit, you won't offend him, but if he's just spending your money talking to the wrong people, you can either move him in a better direction, or move him out."

"Exactly. I've also asked a buddy of mine up in Reno to do some nosing around and check some of his references. I expect to hear from him any day." She looked up the hill ahead of us. "So where is this chicken?"

"Just up there on the right. See the red awning?"

"Got it. Wow, is that smell coming from there? Awesome!" We approached the case that held the rotating chickens and I pointed out the potatoes that were cooking below them in the drippings.

"We *are* getting some of those too, right?" The way Amy said this, it was not a question.

"Definitely. They're incredible." Soon we were on our way back to the apartment, chicken and potatoes in hand.

Sophie and Carol were in the kitchen, and I could smell artichokes steaming.

"That smells great!"

Sophie turned to smile. "And we have an amazing salad as well, including the avocados you requested."

Four people was definitely too many for the kitchen, so I slid by Sophie just long enough to set the bag on the counter. "Watch it. Precious cargo here."

Ten minutes later, we all filled our plates, then headed back to the living room. I put the wine bottle in the center of the table with the breadbasket, and we all sat down. There was just enough room for everything.

"So today was great, though exhausting," said Sophie. "I don't think I've walked that much ever in my life."

"Me neither," agreed Amy.

"That's because you girls live in the west where you drive everywhere. Carol, you walk a lot in Chicago, right?"

"Yes, though today was definitely more than usual! I take the train into work and walk from there, and sometimes walk around doing errands, but it's rare for me to walk this much all at once."

"I don't walk nearly as much as I probably should, either. Was it too much today?"

Carol shook her head. "Not for me. I feel good. Tired, but in a good way."

Amy and Sophie both nodded in agreement. "And as you said, we can eat what we want with all that walking," Amy added. "Like these incredible potatoes!"

I grinned. "Exactly."

"What's the plan for tomorrow?" Amy asked as she reached for another piece of bread.

"Since it's Sunday, there isn't much open, so I thought we'd go to the *Marche aux Puces*—the flea market that's only open on the weekends."

"That's something I really want to do," agreed Amy.

"I think you'll enjoy it. There's a section at the beginning that has cheap clothing and shoes, but past that you get to the real flea market, which is a series of small individual rooms. A different person rents or owns each one, I'm not sure which. Either way, it's my understanding that people occupy the same space for years and years. There is every variety of item you can imagine and a whole lot you can't!"

Amy sighed. "How long can we stay?"

Sophie laughed. "The rest of us will probably get tired of it before you do, but we'll all try to stick it out as long as possible."

"Thanks! When do we go and how do we get there?"

"We take the metro. It's up at the end of one of the metro lines. If we find anything really big, like my chandelier, we can always take a cab back."

Sophie mused, "It's such a different way of doing things. We get so used to just driving over and picking up stuff at home, or getting it delivered."

I nodded. "You're right. Delivery is sometimes an option, but it means having to wait at home. I wouldn't want to restrict our plans during the day. What fun would that be, sitting around waiting for a furniture delivery?" I glanced around at their empty plates. "Looks like everyone is done with the main course. Ready for cheese?"

Carol groaned. "I want some, but I'm so full already."

"Just take little tiny helpings. But you do need to try some."

"I know. I want to, but everything tasted so good, I forgot to leave room."

Sophie and I took the plates to the kitchen. "Can you get the cheeses out, Sophie? They're in the fridge in that little Tupperware-looking thing."

She opened the container. "Whew!"

"I know. Strong, huh? But you know what Dad always says: the stinkier, the more flavorful."

Sophie laughed. "That's why I never ate this stuff as a kid. But I'll try it now, because I'm sure you wouldn't lead me astray."

"That's right, I wouldn't. Here, put them on this plate with a knife, and I'll cut a little more bread to eat them with. We should bring out the butter, too. My French family always served butter with the blue cheeses. I think it mellows the taste a little bit."

We walked back out into the living room, where Amy was looking at the bottom of the wine bottle.

"Looks like we're out," she said. "Do you have another bottle somewhere?"

"Down in the *'cave'*."

"Where?"

I tried to put on my most serious face. "You must realize that when you buy an apartment in Paris, it comes with a wine cellar in the basement, or *'cave'* as it's called here."

Carol's eyes widened. "You're kidding, right?"

"Actually I'm not. Want to go with me to get a bottle?"

"Absolutely."

Amy and Sophie both chimed in. "Us too!"

I went and got my key, and we all walked down the two flights of stairs to the main entryway. "See this door next to the elevator? It leads to the basement where each owner has his or her own space." I unlocked the door and turned on the light by the stairs. Immediately, the cold smell of old stones wafted up. "It smells so good down here. This part really looks like 1890."

Everyone agreed, as we descended the narrow stone steps. "Here we take a right and voila! Here is my *'cave.'*" I stopped in front of the door and unlocked it. "It's about 7 feet wide by about 10 feet long. I've got a couple of suitcases in here as well as wine." I turned on the little battery-operated lantern I kept there, and we moved in next to the bottles stacked on small wooden shelves. "I try to add bottles each time I'm here so I've got a decent number."

Amy asked, "So how do we choose?"

"How about this Bordeaux from 2000? It was a gift from those friends of Mom and Dad's who stayed here last year. It should be good."

Sophie took it from my hands and held it delicately in front of her so the dust wouldn't touch her shirt.

"Sorry. The *cave* has an opening at the back onto the street, so lots of dirt and dust get in here. You're smart to hold it away from you. Everyone else, watch what you've touched because it's definitely grimy."

"But really cool," added Amy. "Okay, back upstairs we go."

We all walked upward and I locked the doors carefully. Once in the apartment, we washed our hands and I took the bottle to the kitchen to wipe it off, then opened it.

Soon we were all seated again.

"Okay. Now, where were we? Oh yes, the cheese course. And now it's had a chance to warm up to room temperature."

Everyone tried a small piece of each of the four varieties I had bought, giving their opinions each time.

"They say France has over 400 varieties of cheese. Hard to believe, isn't it? I'll need years and years to get through them all!"

Amy said, her mouth full, "We would be happy to assist you!"

Carol spoke up. "Time for a toast." She paused while we refilled our glasses, then raised them. "To sisters—people you can talk to about anything."

Amy nodded. "Hear, hear. And to reconnecting—and staying reconnected."

We all nodded and clinked our glasses together.

Carol spoke up again quietly. "And to Mom and her good health. May it last for many years to come."

Everyone clinked glasses again, less raucously this time.

The silence was broken by the sound of a phone ringing.

"What in the world? What time is it?" asked Sophie.

"10:30 at night here, but afternoon at home," I said as I got up to answer. I heard Paul's voice and said, "Oh hi! Checking in on the singles weekend?"

"Sorry to bother you there," he started in his quiet voice. "But I wanted to tell you about something that happened last night."

There was a pause and I could feel my stomach clenching. I took the phone and went into the bedroom, shutting the door. "Okay, so tell me." I sat on the bed, trying to stop my thudding heart. "It's Mark, isn't it?"

"'Fraid so."

"What happened?"

"He went to one of the graduation parties last night and it got busted."

My thoughts were whirling around, a mixture of anger and concern. Mark, our oldest son, was already on probation for marijuana possession. He'd been put on probation for one year instead of jail time because he was underage and it was a first offense. Getting busted at a party was going to jeopardize his already precarious situation.

"All the kids were given warning tickets and told that they would need to appear in court. We're going to have to call his probation officer on Monday."

"Damn it! Why was he so stupid?" I was seething.

"I know…. It's frustrating, but I just keep reminding myself he's a teenager—and it's not like he's the only one. All we can do is continue to remind him of the position he's in and hope that he understands how serious it is." Paul's quiet voice helped to calm me down.

He continued speaking after a moment. "I'll make the calls Monday to the probation officer and to find out when the court date will be." Paul paused. "I thought seriously about not calling you, because I do *not* want to mess up your trip, but then I thought you'd be madder if you found out when you got home."

"As usual, you know me well enough to have done the best thing. I'm mad as hell, but I would have been even madder if I had found out three days from now." I paused, then said quietly, "I'm sorry you're there alone dealing with it."

"It's okay—now." he replied. "Things were tense last night, obviously. But it'll be a little while before we go back to court, and we'll both be here to deal with that. He just needs to figure out how to stay out of trouble until then."

"Yep." I could feel my throat tightening. "Sometimes I wish I could just run away, you know?" I waited a moment to get myself under control. He did *not* need me crying. "That's why this trip means so much—it's my chance to escape, just for a couple of days. I can't tell you how much that means to me and how much I appreciate your being there. Some of the other husbands weren't so understanding."

I could hear the concern in his voice. "I'm *glad* you're over there. This situation has been harder on you than on me. You take all of this so personally."

I added quietly "You are my rock. You know that, right?"

"Feeling's mutual. Go have fun and forget what I told you. As I said, I would rather not have told you, but I did tell you so now you have to ignore it."

"Okay, I'll go back to my wine and cheese, and will see you in a couple of days."

"I love you," he said with quiet intensity.

"I know. I love you, too. See you Thursday. Thank you, my love."

I hung up, then let myself just sit there for a minute, feeling drained. I had found being a parent incredibly rewarding, but had now decided that teenage parenting was officially the hardest thing I had ever done because of the emotional roller coaster it created. Rising, I took the phone and made my way back to the table. Carol and Sophie were laughing at Amy as she was winding up a story about an incident at work. I looked around the group, and felt my throat tighten again. I was so thankful for these wonderful women who, I knew, would be sympathetic and not judgmental if I wanted to spill out my story.

Amy looked up as I got closer. "Hmmm… looks like not great news."

I appreciated her light tone, but the sympathy in her eyes put me over the top.

I found I couldn't speak, but only start sobbing. As I sat in my chair, weeping, Amy and Carol came over to hug me from either side. Sophie quietly got up to get tissues from the bathroom. After a while, I wiped my eyes, blew my nose, and looked up at all of their faces. "Guess it's my turn for a true confession," I said with a watery smile.

Carol said gently. "We are all ears, if you want to talk about it. Or not."

"Actually, I do. I think it would help to say it out loud." I took a deep shaky breath, then started. "Last summer—on my birthday, in fact—we got a call at 2:00 in the morning. We had gone to bed early and assumed Mark would be back by his curfew, which was midnight. He always came in to say goodnight when he got home. Instead, he was standing on the side of the road, next to his car, in handcuffs. Apparently the officer who pulled him over for a burnt-out taillight decided to do a spot car check and found a backpack in his trunk with marijuana in it." I paused. "Of course, Mark claimed it belonged to a 'friend,' but the officer didn't care who it belonged to—just that he was in possession of it, so therefore liable.

I rubbed my eyes, re-living the incident. "By this time, more police cars had arrived with spotlights and even a K-9 dog. They gave him a Breathalyzer test, and the good news was he had not been drinking. The officer told him he could call us to come pick him up at his car rather than them taking him down to County lockup and having the car towed. Small victory, maybe, but a victory nonetheless. So Paul and I drove down there. We spoke to the officers, and then I drove Mark's car home, and Paul drove our car home with Mark. I was so angry and frightened and freaked out that Paul could see that he should take Mark, not me."

"The court date was set for a month later. I don't know about where you live, but where we live, marijuana possession is taken *very* seriously. I was at my wits' end trying to figure out how to proceed, but then realized I had a friend who worked in the sheriff's office. I knew she would be able to give me advice. She gave me the name of a terrific attorney and we took Mark to see him as soon as possible."

Here I actually smiled at the memory of that meeting. "Let me tell you, this guy was great. He scared the holy crap out of Mark. His first words when we all sat down were, 'Well, young man, let's start this conversation by establishing first that you did an incredibly stupid thing, and second, that *you*, not your parents, will be paying my fee.' Mark just looked at him and nodded mutely, clearly out of his depth, and the attorney proceeded with an outline of what would happen from there on. He worked with Mark on getting paperwork from school showing that he was a good student, had him write a summary of his college acceptances, and had him get a couple of character references from teachers. The attorney went to court with us and quietly presented his story to the judge. He argued that Mark was a good kid who generally was moving in the right direction, but had made a dumb mistake. Mark was given a year's probation and a strong lecture warning him not to make another wrong step or the charges would be re-examined and his punishment potentially increased. If he stayed out of trouble for a year, all charges would be dropped and expunged from the court record, since he was a minor." I stopped and took a sip of my wine.

"Then, last night, he went to a graduation party that got busted."

Amy shook her head. "These teenage boys. Dumber than rocks. Mine, too, by the way. So now what happens?"

"Well, they took his name at the party and gave him a ticket, which means another court date." I sighed. "We were *almost* through his year of probation. I was actually thinking we might make it." I felt the tears start to trickle down again. "It feels like we're back to square one, or maybe worse. He's eighteen now, so no longer a minor...."

Sophie spoke up. "I hate to be the one to state the cold hard truth of the matter, but you know, Margot, it's his life, and if he screws it up, well, it's his problem, not yours."

"That's easy for *you* to say," I shot back, frustrated with her attitude. "What if we're talking jail time? How would you feel if it were Bobby or Jeremy?"

Sophie looked defiant for a moment before her expression softened. "You're right. I'm sorry I said that. But it does seem like he should take on the responsibility and not you."

"The worst part is that something like this can affect the rest of your life and *I* can see that, but *he* doesn't seem to have any clue or understanding of that at all."

Carol spoke up. "Does this mean you need to go back early?"

"No. Paul said he would call the probation officer on Monday, and he assumes it will take a couple of weeks for the new court date." I paused, then added, "Better for Mark that I'm here. I'd probably kill him if I were there."

Amy asked, "So is there anything else we can do?"

I shook my head. "No, just talking about it helps." I turned to Carol. "You were right. It's a relief to let it out. Now I know how you felt when you told us about George."

Carol nodded. "I can imagine that this is not something you've wanted to talk about with friends at home."

"Definitely not. We've told a few people, but it's embarrassing. You feel like they're judging you, as well as your kid."

"It's not like you're alone," Carol continued. "You know there are other parents with kids going through various versions of this story or another. My neighbor's daughter is fifteen and pregnant."

I nodded. "You're right. You do start hearing other stories when you confide in people, but until you do, it feels like you must be the only ones. I told the mother of a friend of Mark's, and she then told me stories about her son that were actually worse. But she'd never shared them until I told her about Mark."

Amy looked triumphant. "See? I knew that had to be true. The problem is that we all look around and assume everyone else's life is perfect."

I agreed. "You're absolutely right. Still, sometimes it feels like Mark's screw-ups must be our fault."

Amy shook her head. "C'mon sis, you've certainly learned by now that kids are hardwired a certain way from the start, and if you get one with a wild personality, well, that's just bad luck. You can teach them basic right from wrong, and try to create in them an inner moral compass, but in the end, their behavior will be what it will be."

Sophie shook her head. "I disagree. I think that it's all about how you raise them. We haven't had any issues with Bobby or Jeremy, and I think that's because of their home life."

I felt frustration and anger well up in me. "Oh sure," I said sarcastically, "and Paul and I have done such a shitty job. That's why we have such issues with Mark, right?"

Sophie looked hurt, but defiant. "I don't know why you have problems with Mark. I'm not around to see how you raise him. I'm just saying that we haven't had any problems in our house, and I think Roger and I deserve some credit for that."

I sighed. "You know what? I'm sure you two do a fine job raising your boys. I'm just saying that I think we do, too, and I have enough guilt about this without you adding to it with your attitude. I think you're either just lucky to have calmer kids, or you've managed to scare them so badly they won't misbehave in front of you. Let's see what happens when they get to college and Mommy isn't around all the time watching over their shoulders."

Sophie looked stubborn. "We'll see. I don't think my kids are scared. I think they're good kids."

I almost choked on my wine. "So now you're saying you have angels and Mark is inherently evil? Mark has a strong personality and is very independent. Those aren't necessarily bad qualities. I feel like we've done a good job teaching Mark strong moral values, which, as Amy said, is all I think you can do as a parent. I'm confident he'll grow out of it. In the meantime though, I would say that being a teenager demands good judgment, and frankly, he doesn't have any. It's clear his 'common sense' gene is not wired up yet."

"I'm sure you're right on all counts," Carol said in a soothing tone. "Margot, it's not your fault. I know you know that intellectually. Your emotions are just having a battle with that concept right now. My kids are just a year behind each of yours, and I can see Brian already has a much bigger tendency than Gwen to follow the crowd. I'm definitely keeping a closer eye on him."

"Yep." I nodded. "Carl is calmer than his brother, so I think he'll be easier, plus he's seeing all the trouble Mark's in. Hopefully he's taking it to heart. Now if we can just get Mark through this and off to college."

"The good news is he's been accepted and will be headed out in the fall. Just keep that in your mind." Carol paused. "Heaven knows he's not the first high school graduate to get busted at a graduation party!"

I smiled wanly. "True, but being on probation already makes it much more serious. And the fact that he's now eighteen. I'm terrified he'll go to jail."

Amy said. "To be honest, and I'm not just saying this to make you feel better, I would be very surprised if he went to jail. The fact remains that he's a good kid and that works in his favor. I bet the judge just extends the probation."

"I hope you're right." I got up from the table and started gathering our dishes. "And I'm not going to worry about it for the rest if the trip because there's nothing I can do from here anyway."

Amy raised her glass in salute. "You'll deal with it when you're home, so just let it go and let's continue to have a good time. You'll have plenty of time to worry when you get back."

Sophie spoke up suddenly. "Margot, I'm sorry. I'm sure it will all be fine." She paused. "It's hard for me to say this, but...." She paused again, and when she looked up her eyes were troubled. "I'm afraid I'm *not* doing a good job with my boys. I'm not with them as much as I'd like to be because of all my work obligations and I worry about that. Roger does a great job, but I sometimes feel very out of the loop on their lives. Without that active participation, I feel guilty taking credit for their good behavior."

She cleared her throat. "Right now, I feel like I have too many jobs to do… and I'm not doing *any* of them as well as I'd like. I'm telling you all of this because, to be honest, I'm relieved that we haven't had any problems yet." She looked up at Margot. "As mean as it sounds, it makes me feel better that you've had problems instead of me."

I started laughing. "It's like when someone else gets sick and you feel sorry for them, and at the same time, you feel relieved it's not you."

Sophie nodded before adding, "Look, our families haven't spent time together recently, so I can't speak from direct observation, but I know *you* and, based on that and the time we did spend together when the kids were smaller, you've been a wonderful mom. I don't want to imply anything else. I realize it's my own fears that made me be so harsh. Forgive me?"

I walked over and gave her a hug. "It's okay. We're all dealing with teenagers right now and that means we're all under a lot of stress. I agree with Amy's earlier suggestion that we leave those worries at home and enjoy our time together."

"Let's just get these dishes into the kitchen and watch a movie. What do people want to watch? French Kiss? James Bond? We have a full variety at this establishment!"

Everyone laughed and got up, taking dishes into the kitchen. Carol squeezed me as she went past. Everyone insisted that I sit and relax while they cleaned up.

That conversation had been rough, but I was still glad I had told them. I reminded myself, as I had many times over the past year, that one day Mark would grow up and become a sensible, fun person again. There were certainly a few stories from my own teen years that showed monumental stupidity. I was lucky Sophie hadn't decided to bring up examples of my partying ways at Mark's age—that could have put a whole different spin on the conversation! I wondered, for the hundredth time, how much of his partying was somehow genetic and "my fault." I shook myself. That was not a productive line of reasoning and it didn't change the situation. I could *not* hold myself responsible for *his* behavior on those grounds. He would have to figure out for himself what kind of person he wanted to be. I knew, in my heart, that

we were good parents. But it was *damned* hard to
remember that sometimes....

Chapter 19. Sophie

Sophie woke to the sound of thunder. Reaching over to the window, she pulled it open slightly and pushed the shutter outward to get a better glimpse of the weather. The sky was uniformly gray, though it seemed to be lightening even as she watched. There was a steady rain and she was struck by how musical it sounded as it bounced off the rooftops and onto the cars below. She breathed deeply, enjoying the smell of the wet pavement. Grabbing her watch, she saw it was just 8:30. She had made the adjustment to Paris time!

Getting up, she heard no one else stirring. Turning the corner into the kitchen, she found Margot, standing in front of the espresso machine in her pajamas, deep in thought. Not wanting to startle her, Sophie spoke quietly,

"Hey, you. Good morning."

Margot gave a start and turned, smiling. "Good morning to *you*." She moved forward and gave Sophie a tight hug. "You're up early."

"You too." Sophie returned the hug and then stepped back. "You doing okay?"

Margot smiled. "You know what? I actually am. Talking to you guys last night was such a relief. I slept really well."

"I'm glad. You have a lot to deal with. Thank God you have Paul."

Margot nodded. "I know. He's been a rock through all of this. There have been moments when I wondered if I would lose my cool completely, but he has stayed strong throughout."

"Did that surprise you? He's always struck me as calm."

Margot looked thoughtful, then said, "He *is* very calm. That part didn't surprise me. He's also someone who rarely gets angry. I'm a yeller or a crier in stressful situations. Not Paul. I've only seen him angry a handful of times in twenty-five years of marriage, and even when he's mad, it's a very 'quiet' mad. This thing with Mark put us both in a place we'd never been before and I honestly didn't know *how* he'd react."

"There were a couple of tough moments when he did break down a little, and I have to tell you, that was almost harder on me than the actual stuff with Mark. It was horrible to see how much it hurt Paul—this wonderful, giving man, who deserves only the best. It really brought out the protector in me."

Sophie nodded. "That's a feeling that I think is usually reserved for our kids. You know, the mother lion thing."

"I was *so* angry at Mark for the hurt he was causing Paul. Paul always sees the good in everyone and Mark completely let him down."

"The kids are lucky we have this strong bond with them. We still love them even in moments of crisis."

Margot laughed. "Mark pushed the limits with this one, I'll tell you that." She busied herself with the coffee. "It shows how well Paul knows me that he encouraged me to take this trip. He knew how much I needed to get away."

"You're lucky." Sophie changed the subject. "So what do you have planned for us today? The flea market, right?"

Margot nodded. "Since you're the first one up, why don't you shower and I'll fix your latte so it's ready when you come out?"

Sophie smiled. "You certainly know the way to a girl's heart. My two favorite things to do to start the day: a hot shower and a strong cup of coffee."

"That's something we have in common." Margot held up her own steaming cup, adding wryly, "Last night I was beginning to wonder if we were even related." She held up her hand as Sophie started to protest. "It's okay. I do know how you feel, and I really appreciate that you were willing to add the comment about your own worries. The teenage years are proving to be extremely challenging for me, and I just hope that you and Roger *don't* have to deal with the same issues. Go get in that shower, and I'll see you in a few minutes."

When Sophie emerged fifteen minutes later, combing her hair, Margot was fully dressed and ready to go to the bakery. "Let's get those lazy girls up." Margot started singing an old Girl Scout song and Sophie chimed in loudly.

Thirty minutes later, everyone was seated around the table full of morning delicacies. "How soon do we leave?" asked Amy through a bite of baguette slathered with butter and honey.

"I figure we'll head out right after breakfast," said Margot. "The rain seems to have mostly stopped."

"That's what woke me this morning," Sophie agreed. "The thunder."

"Thunder?" said Amy. "Didn't hear a thing. I have to tell you, Margot, I'm sleeping like a rock here."

"Not as quietly as a rock," chimed in Sophie. "I didn't realize what a snorer you are."

Amy grinned. "Jim used to say that, too. His solution was to nudge me over onto my back."

"Did that work?"

"Not really, but he could then jump on top of me." Margot looked startled. "Just kidding, Margot! Yes, it helped." She continued laughing. "Man, it's so easy to get you! Look at you, you're actually blushing!"

Margot ducked her head. "I'm such an easy target."

"You're not kidding! I have to say, though, I'm glad to see you smile this morning."

"Talking last night really did help. Thanks, everybody."

Sophie took the last piece of baguette, and Margot said, "Let's head out at 10:00. Just as a warning, a lot of the market is outdoors, so bring a sweater if you are worried about getting cold."

"I'm *really* excited about this!" said Amy.

"Are you looking for anything in particular?" asked Carol, as she took a last sip of her coffee.

"Not really, but I know there will be some fun trinket that I will just have to have."

Margot and Sophie looked at each and other and laughed. "We made a pledge this morning that we would restrict you to something that is easily portable. We don't want to be carting whatever it is out to the airport on Wednesday."

"Okay, okay. I'll keep it small, but you know I have to find some kind of cool souvenir of the trip. Carol has her painting. I want something fun, too."

"Agreed," said Margot. "I hope you all find something that reminds you of how much fun you're having. That way you'll be sure to come back!"

Forty minutes later, they emerged onto the street and into a noisy, bustling cacophony of sounds and smells. There were people of all sorts—women in long colorful dresses, men in long, loose overshirts above baggy pants. Small boys slipped between groups of people, shouting and chasing each other. Harried mothers tried to keep up with them. There were the smells of curry and other exotic spices. Bright signs in store windows advertised discounts and special deals.

Margot turned to say, "Stay close and keep one hand on any valuables. This is not the greatest neighborhood, and pickpockets *love* tourists."

They started across the crowded street and were immediately accosted by men of all ages and sizes selling watches, cologne, and belts.

Amy looked around and shook her head. "Why do I get the feeling all this stuff fell off of a truck somewhere?"

Margot kept walking. "Just ignore them. Up ahead we'll go down a couple of these rows that have the more generic flea market stuff—scarves, sweatshirts, and hats. You know, the stuff that can be a good gift for co-workers and kids. Then we'll go on into the permanent stands." They started down the first row and, as they passed a stand with various patterned black-and-white sweatshirts Sophie said, "These look different from anything I've seen at home. I think I'll get one for each of the boys."

"That's what I try to find, too—stuff they'll like but that's different from what their friends have," Margot agreed. Amy bought a sweatshirt for Josh too, and then they moved on down the row.

"Here are some nice scarves—and they're cheap!" said Amy. "I think I'll get several so I've got something for people I've forgotten to buy something for."

"Good idea," said Carol. "Eileen in my office would love one of these, I'm sure." More things were thrown into the carry bag and they continued down the row.

At the end, Margot headed across the street and through a small alleyway. It opened out onto another small street, which they crossed to reach the entry to another small alleyway. "Here we are at the first of many little winding alleys of stuff. See how it has a number up on the wall up there? My suggestion is that if you see something you like, think seriously about going ahead and getting it because it's not always easy to find your way back."

Amy gazed around with wonder. "I can see that I'm going to have a hard time leaving here. Wow. So many stalls, so little time." Mesmerized, she made her way to the first stall. "Hatpins! Like those women wear in the movies from the 30s!"

"You weren't kidding, Margot," Carol said. "There's anything you could imagine to buy here."

"I know. From dishes, to linens, to silver flatware, to furniture, to hatpins! Now that you see the variety, does anyone have a better idea of anything specific they want?"

Amy spoke up. "All I know is that I want to find something I can't possibly find at home—something that will always remind me of this trip. I don't know what it'll be, but I'll know it when I see it! "

"Okay, that's not very helpful. Anyone else? Sophie? Carol?"

Carol shook her head. "I have my painting already, and gifts for Gwen and Brian. I'm just along for the ride."

Sophie spoke up. "I'd love to find something for Roger. Maybe a nice wine bottle opener. He is very proud of his wine collection. And since he's got full care of the boys, he deserves a present, too."

"Absolutely," Amy agreed. "Let's keep an eye out." At the corner, all four wandered into a stall that had a variety of pitchers and dishes. Against one wall, Sophie found a box containing a beautiful wine opener with what looked like a bone handle.

"This is exactly what he would like," she said to Margot. "Can you ask how much it costs?" Margot spoke to the shopkeeper and said, "Forty euros. She also said if we buy more than one, they would be thirty-five each. It doesn't seem like a bad price. She said that these are made of bone and are made by Laguiole, which is a brand known for good workmanship."

"Great. Then I'll take one."

"I'll get one for Paul, too, and then we can push her a little on the price. You can always negotiate on these things."

They left the stand shortly afterward, with two wine openers in their bags.

"Speaking of Roger," said Amy, "Was he okay with your coming on this trip? I know you travel a lot for work."

"Actually, he wasn't. I was telling Margot yesterday—he thought five days was too long and Paris too far."

"But you obviously convinced him."

"Not without a fight." Sophie paused. She moved to a side path with fewer people and turned to face them before continuing, "We were being extra polite around each other and in front of the boys, trying to make it seem like everything was normal. It felt like things had smoothed over pretty well. Then, a couple of days before I left, I went by the house to pick up something I'd forgotten and he wasn't there. No big deal. But the weird part is that when I called him to check in, he said he was at home. I had just left there so I knew he definitely wasn't there."

"Hmmm. That *is* strange. Did you ever find out where he was?" asked Amy.

"No. I didn't know what to say. I didn't want to confront him, so I just didn't say anything."

"Understandable." Amy paused. "What did you think?"

"This is going to sound weird, but I suddenly had the feeling that he was cheating on me."

Amy looked startled. "That's a pretty big leap."

"I know, which is why I feel stupid even saying it out loud. But I don't know, I just have this feeling."

"Do you have any evidence?"

"No, but since then, I've been keeping a closer eye on everything, just to try to figure it out one way or the other."

"What will you do once you find out?"

Sophie was silent for a moment, then looked around at all of them and said, "Honestly, I don't know. I still love him. If he's having an affair, I think I would suggest we go to counseling to figure out what's going on. I've realized that we don't seem to really talk to each other about anything of substance anymore. He's been very involved with the kids and school stuff, and I've been busy building my career." She paused. "It's sad to suddenly feel like you've drifted away from someone you sleep next to every night."

Carol squeezed her hand. "Looking at it from the outside, I think you guys have a good thing going, so I hope you work it out."

"I hope we do, too. It's so bizarre for me to suddenly realize I've been going along in such an oblivious fashion, when I feel like I'm on top of everything."

Amy nodded. "Well, it sounds like you have your next steps in mind. I would just say be careful, and don't accuse him of anything until you have some proof. And, have a conversation about it, not a shouting match."

Sophie suddenly let her feelings surface and looked distraught. "But can I forgive him if I find out he's been cheating? I don't know if I can treat this as a one-time misstep."

Amy reached over and laid her hand on Sophie's arm. "With something as big as this, be sure you think through everything carefully. There's a lot of good stuff in your relationship that's worth hanging onto."

"I know." Sophie was silent, then added very quietly, "But I'm not very good at forgiving."

"You may not have to. And if you find yourself in that situation, well, maybe it'll be good for you. It could even take you and Roger to a new, better place in your relationship."

"Thanks." Sophie looked relieved. "Where did you learn so much, baby sister?"

"I've had a few more hills to climb than you have. I've already had to make some tough choices."

"Who woulda thunk I could learn from the rowdy baby of the family? But I will keep all of your advice in mind. Thank you."

"We'll all hope for a happy resolution to the situation, no matter what you find out," said Carol.

Sophie nodded. "Being away has helped me realize I do love him and I do want to make it work."

"Then that's what you need to hang onto."

They all started walking again, and Sophie went over the conversation in her mind. Voicing her fears out loud had made her realize that she really did want it to work. She missed the conversations she used to have with Roger and vowed to reorganize her schedule as soon as she was home. And she needed to figure out when and how she could broach the subject with him. That would be the trickiest part. Her usual style of problem solving was to address the problem head-on. This issue would take some finesse. Well, she had a couple more days to think of something....

Chapter 20. Amy

Sophie turned the corner and there was Carol, in the first stall on the left. It was filled to overflowing with every kind of fabric imaginable. There were tables stacked with bolts of material, and shelves lining each side. There were baskets of remnants, and heaps of multi-colored folded squares. Near the back were what looked like old dressers, with drawers hanging open and overflowing with more fabric.

"This place is very cool. They have all sorts of material. Margot's in the back." She turned back to the table and continued sorting through what looked like linen napkins.

Amy made her way back to Margot.

"What did you find?"

Margot turned, eyes shining. "Old curtains. Look at this material! It would be a great fabric to cover a chair with, I think. Nice and thick, and it's very French."

"Great color! Almost like champagne."

"Exactly. I don't know anything about covering furniture, but I have a chair at home that needs to be re-upholstered and this would look fantastic."

"Very cool idea. How in the world will you decide how much material to get?"

"They'll make me buy both curtains anyway, so there should be enough. If not, I'll figure out something else to do with it, right?"

"I like that attitude!" Amy turned and pushed further into the back of the shop, then stopped in front of another chest of drawers. Pulling out the top drawer, she checked out a couple of pieces of material, but saw nothing of interest. She closed the drawer and opened the second one. Beneath the top layer, she caught a glimmer of pale pink and reached further in to grasp the fabric more firmly. Pulling it out, she saw that the pink that had caught her eye was actually roses scattered throughout the material. They were all shapes and sizes, entwined with leaves. The fabric was hard to see in the dim light, but it looked like the background was the same champagne color as Margot's curtains. As she unfolded the material, she could see that it had fringe on two sides and she suddenly realized that it was a shawl. It was obviously an old piece; age had muted its colors.

Holding it up, she caught her breath. It was gorgeous, and she knew in an instant where it would go at home. She had an old Victorian couch in her living room, and this shawl would work beautifully draped over the back. She carried it out to the front so she could look at it in better light, and to see if it was damaged in any way. Emerging blinking into the sunlight, she came up next to Carol and Sophie.

"Did you find something?"

"I think so. Look." Amy held up the shawl, and in the brighter light the muted colors of pink and green formed a beautiful, soft pattern on the off white background.

"That is gorgeous," said Carol. "It's a shawl, isn't it?"

Amy nodded. "I wanted to bring it out in the better light to see if it is damaged at all." She held one end, gradually letting the material slip through her fingers as she checked for holes and tears. There was a spot near one corner that looked like it had been torn at some point and meticulously repaired with small, neat stitches, but otherwise it seemed perfect.

"I love it," she breathed. "I really hope it's not outrageously expensive."

At that moment, Margot appeared from the dim interior, carrying her curtains and trailed by a small woman who appeared to be the owner.

"Margot, can you ask how much this is?" Amy held up the shawl. "Please tell her that I don't have much money, but I *have* to have this!"

Margot grinned and turned to the woman. After several minutes of rapid speech back and forth, Margot turned back to Amy.

"I've told her that you love antiques, but you are supporting your son and don't have a lot of money. She likes the way you look, which is very important to her. She wants to know how you'll be using it."

Amy smiled at the woman. "Please thank her for her kind words and tell her that it would be displayed proudly on the back of my couch in the living room." She asked hesitatingly, "Has she said how much it costs?"

Margot shook her head. "We are getting there. Let me see." She turned back and continued her dialogue with the woman. There was much arm waving, and gestures toward Amy.

Margot turned back to Amy. "She is happy to hear that you're not planning to cut it up, and you'll be displaying it where you can look at it on a regular basis. If I'm understanding her, it belonged to her grandmother, so she wants it to be well taken care of."

Amy nodded vigorously at the woman. "Yes, yes, I will take very good care of it."

Margot turned back to the woman. After another moment, the woman walked over to Amy and touched her cheek briefly, then turned back to Margot.

"She says that she was asking 75 euros, but that you can have it for 55 euros."

Amy did a quick calculation in her head and gulped before replying, "Say thank you and that I would love to buy it!" She turned to Carol and Sophie, who had been watching the exchange. "That seems reasonable, doesn't it?"

Both Sophie and Carol nodded.

Amy turned back to the shopkeeper and said, "*Merci beaucoup, Madame.*" Her delighted smile showed Amy it had been worth sounding ridiculous to try to say "thank you" in French. Margot purchased her curtains, and Sophie and Carol each bought linen napkins.

Back on the street, Amy announced, "I'm starving! Can we go eat?"

Margot looked at her watch and nodded. "Wow, how can it be one o'clock already? I know a fun café not far from here. Let's go there."

They followed Margot through the maze of alleyways.

"Here it is," said Margot. "The food is decent, there's a lot of outdoor seating, and sometimes there's live music. Wait here and let me see what I can find." She threaded her way into the restaurant and they could see her talking to a waitress inside. In a moment, she motioned for them to join her and they followed the waitress to a small corner table with four newly cleared spots.

"*Merci, Madame,*" Margot said, and the waitress smiled and moved away, returning with menus and then leaving them alone to decide what to eat.

Everyone ordered salads of various types and wine and beer, and after the drinks arrived, Amy turned to Margot. "I honestly don't know where we would be without you! You've been the best tour guide ever."

Margot was clearly pleased. "But it's just as fun for me," she pointed out.

Sophie said, "Since we seem to have established that this trip is about helping each other and being frank, can I ask you a question, Amy?"

Amy smiled. "Sure."

Sophie chose her words carefully. "We haven't talked much about you and your new company yet. First of all, I'm very proud of you for taking the bold and risky step of starting your own shop. I don't have that kind of courage." She paused in search of the right next words. "But I'm worried, too. Buying that shawl, you seemed more worried than I would have thought about spending 55 euros. What is that, about $70? I'm not saying 70 bucks is not a lot to spend on one thing, but I'm getting the impression it's a bigger deal for you than for the rest of us. Am I right?" she finished quietly, and sat looking at Amy.

Amy sat silent for a moment, looking around at all of them. "Margot and I talked a little about this already." She took a deep breath. "Things are okay for the moment, but Melinda and I had hoped that by now we would be further into the black than we are. Start-up costs have been more than we had planned, and she and I have been pretty much paying the business first and ourselves second, so money has been tight for me." She paused and smiled ruefully. "Having a teenager who eats me out of house and home doesn't help." Everybody smiled, thinking of their own teenagers.

Amy continued. "So, Melinda and I had a discussion about our situation and decided to bring in another partner who could help on the business development side. We asked around and ended up bringing in this guy named Andrew Jacobson. I had heard his name over the years, and he came highly recommended from his previous employer. He was looking for work in a new area because, he said, his fiancée lives in Las Vegas. He brought some cash into the deal, and in his contract he has various benchmarks to hit as the rest of his contribution to becoming a partner. So far, he's doing lots of schmoozing—business lunches and stuff like that, which is all as it should be—but we haven't seen any new contracts." She paused again and a look of worry crossed her face. "Everything should be fine, but I just have this nagging feeling in the back of my mind. I don't know why, but I don't completely trust him. He's a big talker, which I know is part of why we brought him in, but I don't want him to spend our money and then not bring in the contracts. I've asked a friend to check his references. I'm doing it all very quietly and behind the scenes because obviously, if he's doing what he's supposed to, I don't want to interrupt that; but if he isn't, I want to stop that train before it runs away with what little money we have."

Sophie looked thoughtful before speaking. "It sounds like you're going about things the right way. I think it's always a good idea to check, and then double-check, new business partners. When will you find out?"

"Any day now," answered Amy. "I've been watching for an e-mail."

"So you still haven't answered the question completely. How bad are you doing financially?"

Amy shook her head sadly. "It's tough right now, I won't lie to you. Jim gives me some money every month to help with Josh, but it's not much—and the mortgage, as you all know, still comes due the first of each month."

Carol said, "You know, we're all happy to help with that."

Amy smiled at Carol. "This trip has reminded me of that, and I'm very grateful. But I don't want to be 47 and asking my sisters for money. Besides, now that we're all airing our dirty laundry, it's obvious I'm not the only one with money issues. I now know that you, Carol, have a non-working husband, and Margot is potentially losing her job. It may be nutty, but hearing about your having these problems actually makes me feel a lot better. I don't feel like such a failure when I know you guys have problems, too—that your lives are not the total beds of roses they look like from the outside."

Carol said, "There's always another side to every story."

Amy smiled again. "I know I'll get through this, just like I have the various other things that life has thrown at me—or, more correctly, I have thrown at myself."

Sophie said, "I have complete confidence in you."

Amy looked around and raised her glass. "I can't possibly express how much that means to me, honestly."

Everyone clinked glasses. "No more silences between us," said Carol. "And no more not talking to each other. We all need someone to talk to about this kind of stuff. We all need sympathetic sisters with no agendas. Agreed?"

"Hear, hear!" Their waitress, standing near the kitchen, wondered what the four American women were toasting. It looked like they might be sisters. The one ordering the food had certainly spent some time in Paris, to have acquired such a good accent. They looked very comfortable with each other, with an ease that comes from knowing each other for a long time.

Watching them from a distance for a few moments, she felt a pang of envy. Maybe it was time for her to visit her own sisters in Brussels....

Amy looked around at her sisters and felt a rush of gratitude. It was great to be able to confess her fears and uncertainties. She was always hesitant to burden Melinda with one more worry. She'd keep an eye out for that e-mail and cross her fingers that the news was promising. If not, well, it wouldn't be the first time she'd been disappointed in someone. There would be a way out somehow. The hardest part would be the blow to her newfound self-confidence if it turned out that once again she'd chosen the wrong road to go down.

Chapter 21. Amy

Back at the apartment after a crowded ride on the metro, everybody dumped their bags and collapsed in the living room.

"Whew! I'm wiped out," Carol said as she kicked off her shoes and curled up on the couch.

"I'm not used to big city life. It's amazing how tiring it is—all the people at the flea market, then all the people on the train." Sophie plopped into the leather chair with a sigh and adjusted the back. "Now this is more like it. I'm not moving from here for a while... okay, maybe never."

Margot looked around. "The good news is we have no set agenda for the evening. It's five o'clock, so we have a couple of hours to just chill, then we have several food options. One, we could order in pizza or Chinese. Two, we could go back down to the café for something simple like an omelet or steak *frites*. Or three, we could go to the tiny Italian place around the corner that makes its own pasta and has about ten tables. Keep in mind that dinner, if we go out, won't be until 8:30 or so."

"I'd vote for the Italian place," said Amy.

Carol nodded. "That sounds good to me, too."

Sophie looked around from her chair and smiled. "As long as we get to stay off our feet until diner, and the Italian place isn't far, that's my vote, too."

"Okay," Margot said. "I'll call to put our name in, since it's so small. Shall we watch a movie in between? Or do people want to nap?"

Amy spoke first. "I'd like to get on the computer for awhile, if no one else needs it."

Sophie said, "I'd like to close my eyes right here. Amy, do you mind?"

"No problem, big sister," said Amy with her usual good cheer.

Margot and Carol decided to nap before dinner and gratefully headed to their beds.

Sophie settled into the chair with her feet up and her eyes closed. She let her mind wander to thoughts of Roger. Was he cheating on her? And if so, what was she going to do about it? She had thought long and hard and had decided that she needed to know for certain. Okay, so she would have a conversation with him when she got back. Then what? What if he said yes, he'd met someone?

She tried to put herself into that conversation and then step back and look at her reactions. Lots of hurt, for sure. And anger, but at herself as well as Roger. She should have seen he was in need of something that apparently she had not been giving him over the last few months. She had to admit that, and take responsibility for her role in this situation.

On to the next question: how did she feel about him? Did she still love him? Yes, she did. She remembered how stunned and honored she had been when he asked her to marry him. So that meant that she needed to fight for him, and for a return to their former relationship. She would need assurances from him that anything that had happened, or was still happening, would end, but she now felt she could forgive him and move on. Surprised at her own reaction, she realized that her love for Roger overrode any judgmental feelings she had about his actions.

Next question: how was she going to broach this delicate topic? It was certainly possible that she was mistaken and nothing had been going on, and she did not want to create additional contention between them that could worsen the whole situation. But what else might he have been doing that day, when he said he was home but wasn't? They needed to have a conversation; somewhere they could not be interrupted. Maybe she could get

Joan to come stay with the boys while she took Roger to dinner. They certainly would have more to talk about than last time, she thought ruefully.

If things went badly, she would have to fight harder. But if things went well... she knew nothing would mean more than reconnecting physically and emotionally. Choosing a familiar and comfortable spot would start dinner off on a more relaxed note. Yes, that was a good idea.

Feeling satisfied that she now had a plan of action, she looked up from her recliner. Amy was seated at the computer, tears streaming down her face.

Sophie scrambled to try to make the leather chair sit upright. "Amy! What's wrong?" She finally got herself vertical and out of the chair.

"I just received the news I've been waiting for," said Amy shakily. When Sophie put her arm around her, she started to cry harder.

"Well, obviously it's not what you were hoping to hear." Sophie rested her head on top of Amy's and said no more.

Just then Margot walked sleepily into the living room. Her eyes widened and her jaw dropped.

Entering the room right behind Margot, Carol said, "Oh, honey—what is it? Is Josh okay?"

Amy sat up and waved her hands in the air. "No, no, Josh is fine." Sophie ran to get tissues. "I just heard from that guy in Reno I told you about." She looked miserable. "I am so embarrassed. I don't even want to tell you about it." She took a deep breath. "But we're having Honesty Weekend, aren't we?"

"I'll say," said Sophie dryly. "I don't see how you can top my story." She handed Amy the tissues.

"Or mine," said Margot.

"Or mine," echoed Carol.

"Well, okay, I'll just read you the e-mail...." Amy blew her nose, wiped her eyes and began reading out loud.

"Amy, great to hear from you, as always. I've done some digging for you on your man, Andrew, and unfortunately, the news is *not* good. First, on his previous work situation. I took a guy he used to work with out for beers and loosened his tongue a bit. The official story was that Andrew had decided, for personal reasons, to move to Las Vegas. The gossip was that the big boss found Andrew in *his* office after a company party, with one of the secretaries, and they were using the big boss's desk as their very own playground. It was all hushed up, of course, but the secretary mysteriously had a family emergency come up and she left the next day. You can imagine the big boss was happy to tell *you* whatever he thought you wanted to hear to get rid of the guy.

"Second, on the question of his 'personal reasons' for moving to Las Vegas. He's told you he has a fiancée. From what I hear up here, there's no fiancée. There *was* a girl in his life up here, but he broke up with her in a nasty fight in front of a pretty big crowd at a local bar. I've since heard, not substantiated, that the girl may be pregnant. I can see why he'd want to get out of town.

"Third, on the money he gave you to become a partner. He closed a big deal up here about six months ago and I'm sure the commission on that deal was substantial. I'm assuming that's the money he gave you. I don't think he has any other funds left. It sounds like he's a guy who spends everything he makes, so he's probably living pretty lean now, until he gets that next contract and commission. He's the kind of guy who could get in trouble while he's waiting.

"Sorry to throw all of that at you. And don't blame yourself for not finding this stuff out. In public, he has a very good reputation, and you've seen he's a very personable guy. It's just not quite as pretty underneath.

"Let me know what else I can do for you. I think you'd be well advised to gently extricate him from the company and find a new partner. Hope to see you soon. Let me know what else you need. Joe."

Amy was silent, reading the email yet again.

Sophie was the first to speak. "Amy, as Joe said, you can't blame yourself. Sounds like this guy checks all the boxes, from the outside. We all know how tough it is to get the real story on any former employee these days. Everyone's worried about lawsuits. You're lucky you have your friend, who figured out how to dig below that."

"What are you going to do?" asked Carol. From the tone of her voice, it was apparent she was as overwhelmed as Amy.

Amy sighed, then spoke quietly. "As Joe says, I'm going to have to talk to Melinda, and then we'll have to figure out how to get rid of him."

Sophie spoke up in a no-nonsense tone. "That's *exactly* what you're going to do and you will *not* beat yourself up about it. We all make mistakes, and this guy could have fooled anybody."

Amy looked stricken. "*How* could I have been so fooled? Now that he says these things, it all seems like information I should have been able to gather."

"How in the world would you have done that?" Sophie shot back. "You haven't lived up there; you don't know the social scene or business scene like your friend does. If you'd gone up there and nosed around, you would have been patting yourself on the back for your great catch!"

Margot agreed. "He looks fantastic from the outside. *All* of us would have brought him on. This is not a time for looking back. This is a time for moving forward."

Carol added, "You and Melinda have great connections and *will* build the business. It may not happen as quickly as it might have, but it *will* happen."

Amy looked around. "Thanks. You're all correct. I've got to move forward, not wallow in my mistake. I'll send Melinda an e-mail so she knows there's a problem, but I'll wait 'til I'm back to really talk through it with her and sort it out. This is not something to discuss in a phone call."

Sophie agreed. "Two more days of vacation won't make any difference. Let's all agree that you have a plan of action and, like Margot, you'll set this problem aside for the remainder of your time here."

Amy smiled for the first time. "Good advice. It'll be hard not to think about it, but whatever we do will require some careful planning—and talking to a lawyer." She took a deep breath and blew her nose one more time. "I'll go fix my makeup—no one wants to go out with smeared mascara, for heaven's sake—and then let's go eat."

Margot glanced at her watch. "It's eight o'clock. Let's *all* get beautified and head downstairs."

A half hour later, Margot led the way around the corner and stopped in front of a very small green door. "This is it."

Amy looked astonished. "This looks like a narrow entryway to an apartment building. Is it wider inside?"

Margot opened the door and entered. "Nope." She grinned. "But it doesn't need space to be delicious. See that table in the corner? That's where the owner rolls out the pasta."

"Awesome!" Amy breathed deeply. "Smell that garlic? I'm going to love this place, I can tell already."

They were seated at a small table near the back. They each ordered, letting the waitress guide them with her suggestions and explanations. Then they sat back with their wine and watched the owner roll and form the various types of pasta that would be their dinner.

"I can't imagine a restaurant like this in the States," said Amy. "We have too many health regulations. Don't get me wrong," she added hastily, "I'm not saying it's wrong. But our regulations wouldn't allow her to stand right there, ten feet from where we are sitting, making the pasta."

Carol said, "It's too bad, because it creates such a great atmosphere."

Margot added, "It tastes even better than it smells!"

A while later, as they all sipped their espressos, Amy looked around the room and sighed. "Yep, it tasted as good as it smelled. I'm telling you, eating like this would make me as big as a house if I did it every day. How in the world do these French women stay so small and thin?"

Margot spoke up. "If you look at some of the older ones, they're not *all* thin. There is definitely some widening at the waists, even for French women, as they get older—though much less than at home. I don't know the answer, but am convinced all the walking has to be a part of it. Your metabolism stays pumping at a higher level, I think."

"That makes sense," said Sophie thoughtfully. "And I'm assuming French women don't eat pasta like this every day, either."

Margot agreed. "The largest French meal was traditionally in the middle of the day, instead of in the evening, which everyone now says is the healthier way to go."

The conversation moved on to family topics, school, and kids' sports, and Margot sat back and looked around. What a special circle they formed. It was easy to see how they had grown apart with the physical distances between them and all their family and work commitments, but she knew that for her the timing was perfect for this reunion. Being a parent to teenagers demanded a strong, non-judgmental support network. Her sisters had proven they could be both of those things. It felt wonderful to rediscover a source of strength that had been there all the time. She smiled, and as she looked around she got warm smiles in return.

Back at the apartment, Sophie said, "Margot, what's the plan tomorrow?"

"Tomorrow is the D'Orsay museum. No hurry in getting up. We'll just go when people start moving around."

Amy smiled. "Ah, vacation!"

Sophie spoke up. "Why don't you all get ready for bed? I want to call Roger and check in."

Her sisters all looked at her questioningly. "Hey, can't a girl call her husband without having to explain?"

Amy laughed and sang out, "Group hug!" They all huddled together, then went their separate ways, still giggling.

Amy lay in bed, feeling completely drained. Thoughts of Andrew and Melinda came rushing back, and she berated herself again for hiring him. Intellectually, she knew that she had done all she could, but she realized she had been in such a hurry to secure a good partner she had not paid enough attention to her intuition. She should have asked Joe to do the background research earlier. Tossing and turning, she kept going over and over the interview with Andrew in her head, looking for some clue to his real personality.

As dawn broke, Amy finally fell into a deep, troubled sleep.

Chapter 22. Carol

The next morning Margot went into the kitchen and found Amy already there. She had deep circles under her eyes.

"'Morning. You don't look like you slept too well."

"No. I kept re-living my interview with Andrew. You can't always control your brain on these things, you know? I'd love to help with breakfast—take my mind off all that."

"Well, we need to make coffee and get baguettes and croissants. Which would you rather do?"

"I'd like to try to buy the baguettes and croissants, if you tell me what to say."

Margot was pleased. "Great! It's pretty simple really. You start with *'Bonjour, Madame.'* Then say, *'Deux baguettes et deux croissants, s'il vous plait.'*"

Amy looked sheepish. "Can I just hold up two fingers and point, like at the market?"

"Absolutely. Here's four euros; that should be plenty. Do you remember where the bakery is?"

"Just around the corner, right?"

"Exactly. And take the key with you, because it has the codes for getting back in from the street."

"Okay." Amy's eyes gleamed. "This is going to be fun."

"Good luck. Or should I say, *'Bonne chance'*?"

"Didn't you say there was a little store right there, too? I'm running low on Diet Coke."

"It's on the opposite corner from the bakery. Same method: just say *'Bonjour'* when you walk in and you'll figure it out. Take a little more money."

As Margot was getting out the butter, jam, and honey, Sophie came around the corner, looking rumpled and half asleep.

"Where's Amy? She was gone when I woke up."

Margot grinned. "She's buying our breakfast baguettes and croissants."

Sophie smiled in surprise. "Good for her! I wouldn't dare do that by myself."

Twenty minutes later, when Amy came through the front door, the other sisters exchanged looks of relief. Margot said, "That took longer than I thought. I was about to send out the search dogs."

Amy laughed. "It was fun! I kind of got into a conversation with the guy who runs the store. He's about 100 years old, but I think he was hitting on me."

Margot shook her head in mock frustration. "Why am I not surprised?"

"He was a sweetheart. Hey, I bought some more milk, too, while I was there."

"That was a great idea."

All four sat down and started reaching for bread and croissants.

"So how was it, Amy?" asked Sophie.

"A little scary, but fun. I did what Margot told me. I started at the bakery and said '*Bonjour Madame*,' but then I admit I just pointed at the baguettes and croissants and held fingers up to show how many. That place smells heavenly, let me tell you."

Margot nodded. "I know. I'm really not tempted by the pastries, but give me fresh baked bread and good butter and I'm hooked."

Sophie took a bite of her heavily buttered bread before turning to Amy. "And then?"

"Then I went across the street to the little store. It's almost like a Parisian version of a 7-Eleven. You wouldn't believe all the stuff he has in that small space! Anyway, I said '*Bonjour, Monsieur*' as I went in—as you taught me, Margot—and he smiled and I wandered around looking for the *Coca Light*. He was very friendly and tried to make conversation as I was paying. Of course, I couldn't understand a word he was saying. We both just smiled and nodded a lot." She turned to Margot. "I have to say, people here have been incredibly nice."

"That's what I always find, too," Margot agreed. "If you show politeness and a basic attempt at speaking French, you're golden." She paused before adding, "But that may not be why they are always so nice to *you*, Amy."

Sophie reached for another slice of baguette and for the honey. "Before we came, I had heard such horrible stories about rude Parisians, but we haven't seen that at all."

"My only experience of that has been the occasional rude waiter, to be honest. I think it's a reputation that is simply not valid anymore."

Sophie spoke up again. "So, Amy, were you scared to go out on your own?"

Amy looked surprised, before replying. "No. A little anxious that I not offend anyone, but no, I was sure I could make myself understood somehow."

Sophie shook her head. "I couldn't do it."

"Really? You're the gal who makes decisions affecting hundreds of people every day."

"You're right, but what I've realized this week is that I know what I'm good at, and I also know that I'm *not* very good at getting out of my comfort zone."

Amy looked thoughtful. "And I'm the opposite. I've always been the 'leap before you look' kind of person. I'm more freaked out when I have to speak in front of people, or present to people who I'm afraid know more about my topic than I do."

"Public speaking is something I feel like I can do in my sleep." Sophie turned to Carol. "What about you?"

Carol was silent for a minute. "The thing that worries me most is letting people down. At work, for instance. I've been doing what I do for a long time, so I'm usually confident enough, but sometimes I get a nagging fear in the back of my mind that I'm not living up to someone's expectations."

Amy snorted. "You're way too conscientious for that to ever happen."

Margot spoke up. "I totally agree. You seem like you're too self-aware to ever let that happen."

Carol looked thoughtful. "Eileen at my office said the same thing the day I was leaving. I started going on and on about our upcoming annual meeting and she shut me down (nicely, of course) and told me to just start thinking about this trip." She was silent again and, when she spoke, her voice was tinged with sadness. "I think that feeling is woven into this whole situation with George. I know I'm not happy, I know that I should somehow change things; but if I give up on him and actually ask for a divorce, it feels like I'm letting a lot of people down."

"Who?" asked Margot.

"Well, the kids, and myself, and George, and even, in a weird way, our parents, who've been married for fifty years."

"Wow," Amy said with a big sigh. "That's a lot of weight you're putting on your own shoulders for a situation that has been created by George. You know that, right?"

"It still feels like it's up to me to 'fix' it, which is where the possibility of letting people down comes in." Carol paused. "And to top it all off, I also worry about how he will make it financially, if divorce is what this all leads to."

Amy said loudly, "Whoa, there. Why in the world is it your responsibility or worry how he 'makes it financially'? Isn't he an adult? Is he disabled in some way? Is that why he hasn't had a job for so many years?" Her eyes flashed. "Don't you dare take him on as something more *you* need to take care of. He is a full-grown human being and should have the capacity, even if he apparently has no drive."

Carol looked sheepish. "I know all of that in my head, but it's my heart that isn't quite convinced."

Amy breathed out slowly. "Sorry, I just see this most generous, wonderful person, tied to this no-good, lazy, manipulative guy, and it gets me all worked up. Carol, you deserve to be happy and to be cherished. And this current situation is not fair. Unfortunately, the responsibility for figuring out the next difficult steps in your relationship is falling on you. Believe me, I do know how difficult it is to end a relationship, from my own experience four years ago."

Carol nodded thoughtfully. "Do you have any specific advice?"

Amy looked serious. "For Jim and me, it took a particular incident to push me to a point of no return. I knew I couldn't trust him anymore after that. Even though I felt sorry for him, I needed to step back and think about how I was going to create a safe and financially secure place for me and for Josh."

Carol looked grim. "Feeling financially secure is a huge issue for me, too, and this time away from home has made me realize that I haven't trusted him since I found that credit card and learned about the gambling. I have to figure out how to get out."

Amy looked sympathetic. "It's complicated for sure. You've been hovering somewhere in the middle for years, and that feels relatively comfortable. Now it sounds like you've made a choice. But the next steps are going to be very tough. At least you now know you have us and we're behind you a hundred percent."

"Thank you. I'm very grateful for that. Talking about it out loud with you guys has helped me see that the situation is urgent."

Sophie said, "We all want to see you happy."

"Amy, thank *you* for reminding me that you've been through this already. If you don't mind, I'd love to come back to you with questions that come up as I continue to think my way through next steps." Carol looked around. "Let's move on to more fun topics. We're off to a museum, right Margot?"

"Yep, the D'Orsay museum. I like it because it's not overwhelming like the Louvre, it's housed in a wonderful building, and the exhibits are always interesting. That's where the Impressionist paintings exhibit is that Amy wants to see."

Margot directed everyone to the same bus they had taken to get to the Latin Quarter, explaining they would just be riding it further this time. Sophie found a seat and looked out of the window. She knew Margot would tell them when to get off, so she didn't have to worry about that and could let her mind wander. She realized, with amazement, that she had almost completely dropped her usual wariness. Not only was she getting on a bus not knowing exactly where she had to get off, but she was also trusting Margot with directing her. Maybe, at home, she had forgotten how to let Roger take the reins once in awhile. She thought back to the phone call with him last night. It had been stilted at first, but soon they had been talking easily about the boys and, when she hung up, he had even said he loved her! She was more hopeful than ever that they would get through this, whatever "this" was.

Amy turned to Margot. "Margot, how much further?"

Margot answered, "Just a couple more stops. By the way, see all these shops? I think we should come back here this afternoon."

The bus dropped them across a broad street from the museum and they had a clear view of the building itself. An enormous circular window at the top faced the Seine, which sparkled behind them. They turned to watch one of the tour boats float by, and they could hear bits of the tour guide's monologue. As Margot led them across the street she commented, "I'm glad we're a little ahead of the main tourist season—the lines get ridiculous." They were soon at the ticket window, then stepping into the museum itself.

Moving through the vestibule and into the main room, they were assaulted by light.

"Wow, this is gorgeous!" Carol exclaimed.

Margot smiled. "It started life as a train station. Aren't the vaulted ceilings incredible? As you can see, the sculptures are in this open area, and the galleries are on three levels up each side. The Impressionist paintings are on the second floor, Amy, and the third usually has special, limited-time exhibits. Right now it looks like some sort of photography. That could be interesting. Okay, so where do you want to go and how do you want to do this? All together? Split up? Your choice."

Amy spoke up. "I would love to wander together, at least at first. If some of us want to linger and others don't, we could split up then."

They started through the first set of smaller galleries, and Margot stopped in front of a large painting. "Here is one of my favorites." The painting showed an open-air market. There were women with babies and a group of children on the ground, playing some sort of game. "It's called *Age des Ouvriers* by an artist named Leon Frederic."

Sophie spoke up first. "I can see why you like it," she said. "The expressions on the people's faces are fantastic. See that woman? She looks worn out with life. But look at these kids!" She pointed to the other side of the picture. "They're having a great time and, like most kids, seem oblivious to anything or anyone around them."

Carol nodded. "You can tell these are people without much money. Look at the tear on that woman's blouse. But the kids don't seem to be aware, or saddened by that. They're just playing with whatever they can find, having fun."

Margot said, "It's the faces that I really love. Every time I look at it I feel like I see something new."

"I totally get it," said Amy. "Though it's painted more realistically than the Impressionist works that I love, it has the same quality of showing emotions, not just figures."

"I'm glad you like it," said Margot. "It's one of my favorite things to come back to see when I'm in Paris."

Two hours later, all agreed they needed a lunch break. Once outside, Margot led them to a small café that faced the Seine. A small, dapper man with a neat mustache approached in his dark apron and crisp, white shirt.

Carol

"Bonjour, Mesdames." He smiled warmly. *"Vous dejeunez?"*

"Oui," responded Margot. They ordered omelets with *frites,* and beers. When the beer arrived, Sophie lifted hers. "Here's to our wonderful adventure!" They clinked glasses, then Amy spoke up.

"So Sophie, we know you called Roger and had a civil conversation. What do you plan to do next?"

Sophie looked around at all of them, then said, "First, I *do* want to know if he's having an affair." She took a deep breath. "If the answer is yes, my guess would be that it's because he feels something is missing in our life together. And, to be honest, he's right. Our whole relationship seems to have gone missing. I know I'll be angry and hurt, but admitting to myself that the responsibility belongs to both of us is helping me bring it into perspective." She paused. "There is way too much good stuff in our relationship to give it up easily. I love Roger and I want to continue our life together. If our marriage has taken a wrong turn, that doesn't mean we can't get on the right path together again."

"From the sound of your phone call, it seems like there's plenty of room for hope. So how and where are you going to have that conversation?" asked Margot.

262

Sophie blushed. "My idea is to get Joan to come hang out with the kids, tell Roger we're going out to dinner, and then we'll go to The Tabard Inn, which used to be one of our favorite places. We'll have a nice, quiet discussion about this whole thing, and I will be very careful how I ask the question so he doesn't feel I'm accusing him of anything. And if that all goes well, we'll finish dinner and head upstairs to one of their charming guest rooms to celebrate the next stage of our lives together!"

Amy clapped her hands. "You go, girl! I think that's a brilliant plan!"

Carol said shyly, "I like it too." She added, "Look at us. We each have confrontations to deal with when we get home. Amy, you'll have to fire Andrew. And you, Margot, are treading that fine line between angry parent and supportive parent. By now I hope Mark understands that this could affect his future. His college offers could even get rescinded—who knows?"

Margot nodded. "It's now very clear to me that teenagers literally are not capable of understanding the long-term consequences to short-term stupid teenage actions."

Carol continued, "And I've got to talk to George. I've let this situation float along for way too long."

Amy spoke up. "This *is* a crisis moment for all of us right now. Good timing, in a funny sort of way, coming together like this." Suddenly her eyes filled with tears. "I am so thankful for you all."

Margot looked around. "And I love you all."

Sophie lifted her glass. "To sisters—to strong, wonderful, incredible sisters."

They all lifted their glasses in a silent toast.

Amy wiped her eyes. "Enough of all this serious stuff! We're in Paris, for God's sake! What fun thing are we doing next, Margot the Tour Guide?"

Margot laughed. "Well, I'd love to go shopping, if people have the energy. Or we could take one of those boat rides down the Seine."

"I notice you haven't suggested the *Champs Elysees*," Amy said with a questioning look. "I feel like that's the one thing everyone mentioned when I talked about this trip. From what I hear about it, it's all about Gucci watches and Louis Vuitton wallets, and I can't afford either of those things. But the books emphasized that area as a 'must see' part of any itinerary."

"You're right. I don't like that area—it's too touristy and too expensive. Now, that's not to say I don't like shopping. I just like to go where there is a good selection for less money. And it so happens that we can find just that within a couple of blocks of here."

"Sounds good," said Sophie. "Let's go!"

Ninety minutes later, Margot herded them all onto the bus with their bags, where they settled into seats with sighs of relief.

Margot knew they had transitioned into the Parisian lifestyle when Carol said, "I'm going to assume 8:30 is dinnertime?"

"*Bien sur!* And I've got a fun last local spot to show you."

When Margot opened the door of the restaurant, they could smell garlic, baked potatoes, and grilled meat.

"This place is called the Clown Bar. See all the clown pictures?" Margot pointed around them.

"These confirm that I still think clowns are kind of creepy," said Carol.

"I never knew you felt that way," said Margot.

"I haven't been to a circus since the kids were small and I'm totally fine with that."

"Well, hopefully you'll like the food and that'll compensate for creepy clown pictures!" Margot said.

The waitress came over and this time everyone ordered for themselves, with much smiling and pointing at the menu.

The first courses arrived and, as everyone ate, talk turned to the purchases of the day.

"Sophie and I found a great clothing store," said Carol. It was organized by color rather than size, which I'd never seen before. I found a great jacket and blouse for work in my traditional colors of dark green and brown. The most interesting purchase was Sophie's. She found a beautiful white jacket with a leaf design on the sleeve edges in *orange*! Can you believe Ms. Conservative would actually buy something with orange on it?"

Sophie laughed and said, "It's definitely not something I would ever have bought before! But it's perfect."

She continued. "This trip is making me think differently about a lot of things: my home life, my makeup—or lack thereof—even my attitude toward trying new things! Maybe it's time to step out a little. Maybe it's time for a 'new me'!"

Margot raised her glass. "A far cry from the girl we knew in high school who spent weekends in front of the television. Let's toast the new Sophie!"

That evening, as they walked home, Carol found herself thinking back over the conversation at dinner. She loved seeing Sophie's new confidence and she applauded her decision to try to makes things work with Roger. In some ways, it made her own situation that much sadder. She would love to fool herself into believing that she and George could make things work again. The idea would fit in so much better with her constant desire to "fix" everything so no one got hurt.

But, damn it—this time she wanted to be selfish. She wanted to fix the situation in a way that benefited *her*! Was that so awful? She always worried about letting people down. But in this case, she'd let *herself* down. Right there, right then, she decided she was not going to sacrifice her own happiness anymore.

Carol felt a surge of energy at her newfound attitude. She was shocked at the strength of her feelings of anger and rebellion. And there was something else, too. Could it be... optimism? She envisioned a new, tidy home for herself and the kids, with no constant tension and no more walking on eggshells. She told herself she was too young to feel like life held no more potential for adventure or excitement.

Maybe it wasn't just Sophie who would go back home with a new confidence. Maybe it was a life-changing moment for her, too. Could she hold on to those feelings and become a new Carol?

Chapter 23. Margot

The next morning, Amy grabbed Sophie and took her along to buy the baguettes and croissants, insisting loudly, "I need to expose Sophie to new experiences to bring her further out of her conservative shell." I made the coffee, Carol set the table, and soon all four of us were once again tucking into a large basket of sliced baguettes and croissants.

I was the first to speak. "So today is our last full day. I just want to say this has been a *great* trip for me. Thank you all for making the effort to come such a long way to my 'hood.'"

Amy sighed. "I can't believe it's almost over."

Carol smiled and said, "We've all learned a lot about ourselves and about each other, that's for sure! And about *food*!"

"We all agree to send updates after we get home, right?" Sophie asked.

"Absolutely," I said. We all raised our glasses in a silent promise.

Amy reached over to take another slice of baguette. "I have to say, on a different note, I'm really going to miss this bread and butter. I don't eat butter much at home and this is so delicious!"

"I found butter for sale at home that was labeled 'French butter' and got excited," I said, "But it doesn't taste the same." She smiled at Amy across the table. "Clearly, you'll just have to come back!"

"So, Margot, how are we finishing this wonderful adventure?" asked Sophie.

"The Marie Antoinette exhibit. I went ahead and bought tickets ahead of time because I knew it would sell out. It's in the *Grand Palais*, which is a gorgeous building built at the same time as the Eiffel Tower. It just reopened after a major renovation and this is the first show."

I took a last bite of baguette. "Let's clean up the kitchen and head out. We've got to catch the metro over to the *Grand Palais*, and I want to show you the building itself before we go into the exhibit.

Amy asked, "Will there be some of Marie Antoinette's dresses?"

"I hope so. You'd think her clothing would be part of the story, right?"

Sophie added, "I bet they're tiny! People were so much smaller back then."

"Will there be explanations in English?" asked Amy.

"Absolutely. They'll have guidebooks in several languages, I'm sure. This exhibit is a big deal."

Carol had been silent through this exchange and now spoke up quietly. "Margot, I hope this doesn't cause a problem, but could I possibly stay here while you guys go to the exhibit?"

"Sure," I said, concerned. "Do you feel okay?"

"Fine, I just feel a little overwhelmed by all we've done, and was thinking I wouldn't mind a little time on my own." She added, "And your apartment is so comfortable. It's a great place to sit and work out the problems of the world. Or my own problems! I have to admit, now that I'm really thinking about getting divorced, I feel overwhelmed."

"No problem, big sister. Will you be okay alone? Let me find my second key in case you want to go out for a cup of coffee or something." I returned a couple of minutes later and handed the key to Carol. "Remember how the key turns to lock the door?"

Carol nodded. "I probably won't use it because I think I'll just sit here, but it's good to have just in case. Thanks."

"Alright, then. Carol, we'll pick up an exhibition catalog for you. Ladies, let's get out of here!"

As I took them down the stairs of the metro, a warm waft of air brought the smell of close-packed bodies and a slight, underlying smell of urine. Amy said, "I don't know if I'd want to take the metro in, say, August...."

"Yeah, it does sometimes smell a bit, depending on the station and the general temperature, but it's definitely the fastest way to get around the city and I've always felt it was very safe, too. Trains come every couple of minutes and you can see that every kind of person uses it, from businessmen to students to moms and their kids. Buses are much more pleasant because you can see where you're going and enjoy the view, but traffic can be brutal.

"The underlying smell down here reflects an unfortunate reality of life in a big city, and that is that for some people, this is the warmest and safest spot to sleep."

There was silence as we each thought about living in that world. Somehow, our problems didn't seem nearly as serious when viewed in that context. As we pulled into our stop, I stepped forward to pull the latch and unlock the door.

As we walked up the stairs out to the street, Amy commented, "It looked like you actually pulled that latch up on the door to open the metro door. It isn't automatic?"

"No. The doors on the trains here don't open automatically like they do at home. I've seen tourists look panicked when the train stops and the doors don't open, but usually someone nearby notices and unlatches it for them." We stepped out into the sunlight and stood at the lower end of the *Champs Elysees*.

"You asked for the *Champs Elysees*, Amy. Now you get it!" I exclaimed. "See over there? There's *L'Arc de Triomphe,* and to our right is the *Place de la Concorde*." I swept my arm in a wide arc encompassing both monuments.

"Cool!" Amy quickly took some photos. "Now I can say I've seen them!"

"I did feel guilty thinking you'd have to tell people you went to Paris and didn't see those. I just find it really touristy, so I don't come over unless there's a good reason."

"You can see it was designed as a beautiful, elegant, broad avenue, but it's always jam-packed with people. The worst part is stuff like McDonalds. I mean, really—who in their right mind would go to Paris and then go to a McDonalds?"

"I can see why," said Sophie. "Think of it as comfort food for people who haven't traveled much."

I looked at her doubtfully. "I guess I can see that, but still, French food is one of the big attractions. The bread, the butter, the cheeses— everything!"

Amy smiled. "I heard they serve beer at McDonalds. Is that true?"

"Yes, maybe that's the draw!" I answered. "The *Grand Palais* is right over there. I want to show you the building itself first, before we go into the exhibit."

"This street is called Avenue Winston Churchill. And the Metro stop was Franklin D. Roosevelt. Why the American names?" asked Sophie.

"Those streets were renamed in the mid-1940s to honor people who helped the French in World War II."

I led them around the corner and up to a pair of large glass doors that were closed and locked. "Take a look at the enormously high glass ceiling and all that ironwork! That is what I was telling you about before. This was built in 1900 for the World's Fair, like the Eiffel Tower, and was also designed by Gustave Eiffel. See how the ironwork looks the same?"

"You're right. What a great place this would be for a huge formal ball!" Amy's look turned dreamy and faraway. "I can just imagine the ball gowns, and look—the orchestra would be set up right over there."

I smiled. "That *would* be fun!" We all gazed into the space in silence, imagining a grand ball with elegantly dressed men and woman, before I spoke again. "Okay, let's go back around the corner and into the exhibit."

Our next ninety minutes were spent admiring all aspects of the exhibit. There were beautiful gowns from the various periods of Marie Antoinette's life, as well as an amazing array of fine silver and china. We all agreed that life in those days had been very sophisticated on the surface, but underneath it was hard for everyone. Reading the plaques next to the various exhibits, Marie Antoinette and her peers seemed amazingly oblivious to the plight of the lower classes and their issues, but we had to admit they seemed to also have plenty of problems to deal with in their own daily lives.

"I'm worn out," I finally admitted, after getting a catalog for Carol. "Let's go get coffee at a café before we head home."

Amy said sadly. "It could be our last café stop—and I've just learned how to ask for *Coca Light!*"

Everyone looked sad for a moment, but then Sophie added, "This time."

Amy smiled. "Good point! Maybe we can make this a regular event?"

I motioned them forward. "There's a café down here that has a nice view of the river and it's away from the crowds."

"Sounds nice," said Sophie. "I'm a little tired of being around so many people."

As we walked, I tried to point out the landmarks. "That is the *Tuilerie Gardens,* and up there at the end of them is the *Louvre.* We really should go there next time."

"What a huge building," said Amy. "I'm sorry we didn't get there, but I also know that I would have been overwhelmed."

I said, "I haven't been in a couple of years, but when I do go, I choose one exhibit or area to look at so my brain doesn't explode. But it's a museum like no other!"

"Well," Amy mused, "When you stay here for longer periods, which I'm assuming you will one day, you can just go whenever you want to."

I smiled happily. "I can't wait!"

We approached the café and chose chairs facing the river. "These give us the view, but with this plastic on the sides and the awning overhead, we should be okay even if it decides to rain a bit," I said. "What does everyone want?"

Coffees were ordered and talk turned to our upcoming flights the next morning. It was obvious that our minds were starting to turn back to home and the people and obligations we'd left behind. Everyone was quieter than usual.

I said, "I have an idea. Let's engage in some retail therapy on our walk home—of the window shopping variety." We set off down the street. "This is the *Rue Faubourg Saint Honore,* a street known for its boutiques and fashion designer clothing. It's a very ritzy area." I continued. "When we're tired, we can catch our bus home."

For the next half hour there was much speculation about who would buy what if we had the money, and banter back and forth about people's tastes in clothing. We left the designer boutiques and started up the *Rue de Rivoli.* I stopped in front of a set of glass doors. "By the way, this is *BHV,* our department store. Paul and I bought several of our lamps here for the apartment. It's got different stuff on each floor—housewares, stationery, tablecloths, appliances—basically almost anything for the home."

Amy immediately moved to the door. "Stationery from France would be something different for the gals back home."

We continued our discussion about who would buy what as we visited the various floors. On the kitchen appliance floor, we all agreed that we had never seen so many varieties of espresso machines, in so many colors. In the end, Sophie bought a flowered tablecloth from Provence, Amy bought stationery for her friends, and I bought some note cards for Carol so she wouldn't feel left out.

As we went out the door, Sophie spoke. "I'm reaching the end of my walking power. Did you say the bus runs along here?"

I nodded. "Absolutely. There's a stop right there." After a brief wait, we climbed aboard and the bus ride passed in companionable silence.

I looked out the window and thought about everything we had discussed these past few days. As Amy had said, we had all learned a lot about ourselves, as well as about each other. I hoped Carol had enjoyed her time on her own and had not been too lonely. Though I felt she had become less cautious and timid on this trip, I was sure she hadn't ventured far from the apartment. Oh well, hopefully the stationery and the catalog would make up for missing the exhibit.

Chapter 24. Carol

Carol sat for a moment, relishing the silence around her. She had loved these days with everyone, but the silence and solitude were exactly what she needed. She sat in the living room, letting her mind wander to George. What was she going to do?

Amy had certainly made her feelings clear, and all three of them felt she was being exploited. Carol felt betrayed, after the discovery of the credit card and, more importantly, the gambling behind it, and she knew she would never respect George again. But the logistics of getting a divorce seemed so difficult. The kids... The house.... Where to begin? Well, she reasoned, why not take a walk to clear her head? She had always found it easier to think when she was moving.

Sticking some money and a credit card in her coat pocket, she grabbed the key and headed out. By the door she noticed a small map and she put that in her pocket as well. She wasn't planning to go far, but it never hurt to have a map.

Emerging from the courtyard, she took a deep breath and headed to the right, following the path they had taken coming back from the restaurant the first night. She walked slowly, taking in the sights and smells around her. There was a young mother with her small toddler in the park, and she smiled, thinking about her own children and how quickly they'd gotten big. She had memories of them at that age, but it seemed a lifetime ago. She looked all around her, taking in the various storefronts and restaurants. She was struck by what a nice neighborhood this was, rather than a touristy area. Looking ahead she saw the large monument that stood in the middle of the Bastille circle, and she knew that if she turned right she would pass the restaurant from that first night. She smiled, thinking again about how good the food had been and how they had all been so full afterwards.

As she walked, Carol reviewed the various conversations and the problems that each of them were facing, and she realized it was comforting just to know that even these accomplished, strong women were vulnerable, too. She was not the only one whose life was not perfect.

Coming out of her thoughts, she looked around and realized she was standing in front of the archway near the café where they had all had their first drinks. Drinks they had shared with Jean-Michel. She admitted to herself that though she had not purposely come here, her mind had been planning to return all along.

Suddenly he was there, beside her.

"*Tiens.* Look who has come back to visit." His voice was soft and his eyes were smiling.

She blushed. "Well, hello."

"Where are your beautiful sisters?"

"They are all at the Marie Antoinette exhibit."

"And you? Why are you not with them?"

"I don't know. I decided to take a walk instead, and then I ended up here." She looked at him quickly, then looked down. It was true, but it really sounded silly when spoken out loud.

He reached over to gently tilt her face up. "I am so glad you did. Would you like to join me for some coffee or some wine?"

She looked at him and nodded. "Yes, that would be nice. But are you sure you can? I didn't mean to interrupt you."

"Remember, I am my own boss. I can have coffee or a drink whenever I like." It took Jean-Michel just a few minutes to pile his paintings onto a hand truck. She used it as an opportunity to take another look at them, and she was struck again by the emotion each held.

Jean-Michel guided her to the café. He reached over and pulled a chair out for her, then sat down next to her. His closeness made her skin tingle and she could feel his warmth where his arm brushed hers. "What would you like?"

"What are you going to have?" Her voice sounded breathless, but she wasn't able to change it.

"I think I will have a glass of wine. And you?"

"Okay, I will too. Could you choose it?"

"Yes, of course. Red or white?"

"I think white."

"*Bien.*" He motioned to the waiter and quickly ordered, then turned back to her. "I hope you do not mind. I also asked him to bring us some cheese and bread. I did not have lunch today."

"That sounds very nice." They sat in silence for a moment, then he turned to face her. His English was heavily accented, but very good. "I am very glad you returned. I enjoyed meeting you and your sisters and have been thinking about you since then." He paused. "You will think I am crazy, but I felt a special attraction to you that day." He reached over to take her hand. "I do not want you to think that this is something that happens to me every day. It does not. I have learned, in life, that this feeling does not happen very often." He looked at her seriously and was silent for a moment. When he continued, his voice was quieter, and she leaned forward to hear him. "I have been lonely since my wife died seven years ago, and I have been tempted to find comfort sometimes. I will not deny that." At this he turned and looked deeply into her eyes. "But I want you to understand that this is not what I am feeling with you. I do not know what it is. There is a sadness in you, a deep well of pain, but also so much goodness. It reaches out to me. Do you understand?" His look was pleading.

She smiled and squeezed his hand. "I do understand." She looked away for a moment, then turned back to face him. She smiled, and her eyes were warm. "I think it's crazy that you could have this feeling for me, but what is crazier is that I have the same feeling about you. In the brief time I have known you and spoken with you, you have somehow made me feel so good and so alive. I don't understand it at all."

His grip on her hand tightened, but he remained silent as the waiter returned with their wine glasses, the plate of cheeses and a breadbasket. People continued to pass by, but for Carol the world had narrowed to their two chairs. She was oblivious to anything other than Jean-Michel's fine hands, his handsome profile, and his brown eyes gazing at her. They were both silent as they picked up their wine glasses, and Carol felt warmth flowing through her as she reached over to gently tap his glass with hers in a toast. She did not know what she was doing here, but she did know that it felt right and good, and that she had not felt this alive in a very long time.

Jean-Michel cut a small slice of cheese, placed it on a tiny piece of bread, and held it to her mouth. She took it, and as she savored the intense flavor, she asked, "This is wonderful. What is it?"

"It's called *Saint Emilion*. It is from the mountains of Savoyard. Please, take a sip of your wine while the flavor is still in your mouth. You will see, it changes the flavor a little, yes?"

Carol did as he suggested and nodded. "It does. There is a very interesting aftertaste—kind of nutty."

He nodded. "I'm glad you like it. It has been one of my favorites since my childhood." He smiled. "I think perhaps you must have ancestors from France." He fed her another bite.

"Did you grow up in that area?"

He nodded.

"And what brought you to Paris?"

"School. Then I stayed to work here. And by then I had met my wife. She was from Paris and wanted to stay close to her family."

Carol was silent for a moment. She hesitated, then asked, "Do you have children?"

Jean-Michel shook his head sadly. "My wife was not able to have them. It was a disappointment in her life. And in mine." He clapped his hands suddenly and smiled. "But I do not want to think about the past right now. I want to enjoy the present, with you." He reached over to brush her hair off of her forehead.

His touch was warm, and Carol found herself leaning into it for a moment before pulling away. What was she doing? She was a married woman with responsibilities. And children, her conscience whispered. But her romantic side was reveling in this moment. She felt as if an important part of her was waking after a deep sleep.

They finished the cheese and their wine, talking comfortably about life in Paris and some of the sites Jean-Michel loved to visit. When the waiter took their plates away, Jean-Michel turned once again toward Carol. "I have enjoyed this time with you."

Carol nodded. "Me too." She noticed that she was holding his hand, and realized that she had been for some time. He glanced down and smiled at the sight.

"You have beautiful hands."

Carol blushed and looked down. She wanted to say, "So do you," but that seemed too forward.

Jean-Michel paid the bill and it was time to leave. Carol realized she did not want to move from this place or from this special moment in their private world. Jean-Michel helped her to her feet, then continued to hold her hand as he led her across the street. "It has been a slow day for me today. The weekends are much busier, with so many more people. I was just thinking of leaving when you arrived." He paused, then turned to fully face her. His body was aligned fully with hers, only inches away. She could feel the electricity between them. "I know this is foolish for me to ask, but would you consider coming with me to my apartment?"

It was a simple question, simply asked, and it held so much promise and so much risk. Carol felt at a loss to speak. A furious battle went on in her mind. How could she even consider saying yes? She didn't know him. He could be a murderer for all she knew. She was a married woman. She was American and he was French. She was feeling vulnerable, and should not let herself be taken in by the kindness of a stranger.

In the end, there was no need to answer. He didn't say anything, just reached out and put his arm around her waist. She yielded to his warm grip, and placed her head on his shoulder. He smelled wonderful, of musky cologne. Her worries evaporated as she closed her eyes and leaned against him. He closed his eyes for a moment and smiled.

Side by side they walked around the corner. In silence they turned into a small street and proceeded until he stopped at a large wooden entry door not unlike Margot's. Still in silence, she followed him into the cool darkness of an ancient courtyard, and he led her by the hand to another door. He stood aside to let her through. She knew she was supposed to be nervous, yet she was not. Jean-Michel led the way up one flight of stairs to a wooden entry door. He pulled out a key, and as the door swung open, he gestured her forward with a gentle smile and a warm look. She stepped through and gasped. Everywhere there was light—and pictures! It was like a museum just for her. Here was an old woman hanging up the wash on a clothesline; there was a man sitting quietly on a bench next to the river; and over there was a young boy playing with a bright red ball in a park. All around her were scenes of Paris, and she was sure they all showed real people in real moments of their lives.

"These are wonderful!" She moved slowly from one to the next. She walked around the room, and as she stood in front of the last one that brought her back to where she had started, she felt him behind her. His arms came around her and then he turned her gently and bent to kiss her. The world dissolved and all she could see and feel was him— his soft, warm mouth, his hands reaching around to encircle her. She held herself separate for a moment, then let the emotion carry her away. Her own arms encircled his neck. His breath tasted of the wine they had both drunk. She felt like she was floating above the whole scene, looking down at the two of them. The practical, moral side of her moved to the background and her emotional side, which had become encased in a hard shell of self-preservation, melted with his kindness and soft kisses. When had she last felt the stirrings of a deeper warmth growing inside her? She willingly stopped thinking and simply let herself feel, as Jean-Michel's kisses became more urgent and he moved her toward a door at the far side of the room. As he lowered her gently onto the bed, she willed herself to be brave and open her eyes, to truly savor the moment instead of removing responsibility by keeping her eyes closed. His smile and gaze were almost more than she could bear, and she felt her heart swell with the wonder of his simple goodness.

"This is crazy," she whispered. "Is it wrong?" She looked briefly worried.

"*Oui, ma chere*, this is crazy," he whispered. "But not wrong." He kissed her and she let herself go, drowning in the feel and smell of him, letting time and the real world fall away.

****

Carol woke slowly and realized that the weight across her chest was Jean-Michel's arm. "What have I done?" she asked herself in wonder. She was glad to realize she did not feel any guilt, but just remembered pleasure. Her movement, though slight, woke him and he lifted his head to gaze at her. "*Bonsoir, ma chere*."

"*Bonsoir*," she replied, testing the feel of the unfamiliar word coming out of her mouth. She came back to reality with a jolt. "What time is it?"

"It is six o'clock."

Carol sat up, seeing her clothes lying in a heap on the floor. She gazed at them for a moment, and then turned toward him. "Thank you. *Merci*."

He smiled at her. "You do not need to thank me for anything. It is I who must thank you for this time together. You may not believe me, but I have not… how do I say this?… been with a woman for a long time. You have reminded me of what it can feel like when two people connect in every way."

She smiled gently. "For someone who claims not to know English very well, you have just said exactly the right thing."

"I think this afternoon we found a language that we speak well together, no?" His smile showed his beautiful, even teeth.

Carol laughed out loud. When was the last time she had felt so carefree? How seldom she laughed at home anymore. She turned back to Jean-Michel and reached over to kiss him gently. "You have made me feel like a beautiful woman again, and I thank you for that."

His look turned serious. "You *are* a beautiful woman. Do not ever forget that."

"I do not want to *ever* forget. Every time I look at your wonderful painting on my wall, I will be reminded of you and of this afternoon." She started pulling her clothes on and, when she had finished, turned to look at him. He was still lying with his head propped on one hand and his smile was incredible. So warm, so soft, and so genuine that it made her heart swell. She made herself pause to savor the moment.

He jumped up suddenly and with an apologetic look said, "Forgive me! I was enjoying the view so much that I forgot to get dressed myself. Give me one moment." He quickly led her to the door of the apartment, down the stairs, and out onto the street. As she emerged into the late afternoon sunlight, she felt the whole world must be able to see how she had changed. For her, everything looked different—brighter, crisper. He took her arm and at the corner, pulled her to face him. He looked at her silently for several moments before saying, "I want you to know that I feel very blessed to have had this time with you. I think we have something special between us and I want you to promise me that you will remember our time together. I know that you have a full life of your own, but I can tell that you have problems, too. I hope you will remember me as a special moment in the special city of Paris, and that you find the answers you are looking for."

He searched her face and seemed to come to a decision. He reached into his pocket and pulled out a small piece of paper. "I have written my information on this paper. I would be very happy if you would write to me sometime and maybe come back to see me."

Carol leaned toward him to kiss him lightly on the lips and took the paper gently from his outstretched hand. She felt her throat close with the emotions she was feeling for this wonderful man whom she did not know at all, but knew so well. She said, huskily, "I promise you that I will keep my memories of you in a most special place. Thank you for your generous gift of your art, and of yourself. You have made me feel special, and that alone has helped me find the answer to my problems." She reached up and kissed him again. "*Merci,* Jean-Michel. I cannot promise I will write, or come back. But I feel that life may bring us back together." She reached over to stroke his cheek. "Until we meet again."

She turned and began walking slowly up the street, pausing just once to look back to wave. He was watching her walk away. He lifted his hand, then slowly turned to make his way back the way he had come. She continued, filled with a sense of wonder that this wild, crazy thing had happened to *her* of all people—the quiet, conservative woman who kept all of her life in neat, organized boxes. She wrapped her arms around herself and smiled, thinking about what her sisters would say if they ever found out. Would she tell them? She didn't know. She would let whatever happened happen, just as she had this afternoon. It felt weird for her to take such a relaxed attitude, not to worry or try to control every eventuality. She wanted to keep this carefree, relaxed feeling when she returned home. And she had Jean-Michel's painting to remind her.

Picking up her pace, she hurried back to the apartment, hoping to arrive before her sisters got back.

Chapter 25. The Mitchell Sisters

As they approached the apartment door, Amy spoke. "I hope Carol's okay. It would be a bummer to get sick right before heading home."

"I think she was just tired," responded Margot. "It's been a great few days, but I know for me it's been physically and emotionally draining, too."

"I agree," said Sophie. "Soul-baring is exhausting, especially if it's not your normal behavior, you know? These few days have made me realize how private I am about stuff at home."

Margot opened the door and called out "Carol?"

Silence. "I guess she did decide to go out." Looking at her watch, Margot added, "It's 6:30, so I figure we have a couple of hours before we need to get our 'last supper' together. We can pack, sleep, watch TV, whatever." Just as she finished, Carol walked in.

"Well!" Amy smiled. "So you did decide to take a walk?"

Carol nodded. "My thoughts kept turning in circles, so I decided to get out to see if I could move my thoughts forward."

"Did it work?"

Carol nodded, blushing slightly. "Very well, thank you."

Amy looked more closely at Carol. "And where exactly did you walk to?"

Carol looked away for a moment, then back at them, and they could all see that her eyes were sparkling, though she seemed uncomfortable as well. "Well, I started by wandering in the general direction of the restaurant we went to that first night.

Amy, with a glitter in her eye, said, "And? Then?"

Carol grinned. "Well, then, I kept walking, and somehow I ended up at the café where we had drinks that first day."

"Well, that's interesting," drawled Amy. "See anyone you knew there?"

Carol was silent a moment, before looking at them with a spark of defiance. "Since it's Honesty Week, yes. Jean-Michel. It turns out he is from the Savoyard area and he introduced me to one of his favorite cheeses and an incredible white wine to drink with it."

Amy's look became more penetrating. "What else did he introduce you to?"

Carol laughed suddenly, her newfound, carefree feelings bubbling over. "Amy, you're impossible! I was thinking all the way back here that I could just tell you I'd just had a glass of wine with him, and that would be fine. But you aren't going to let me get away with that, are you?"

Amy shook her head vigorously. "No chance, honey. Full disclosure. So?"

Carol looked around at all of them and let out a deep sigh. She didn't say anything for a moment and her look became serious. "I went back to his apartment," she said quietly. There was a short pause before everyone started talking at once.

"What? You went to his apartment?" said Sophie, looking both angry and disbelieving. "Are you nuts? You don't know him at all. He could be a murderer, or who knows what!"

Amy smiled and shouted, "You go, girl!" reaching over to give Carol a high five.

Margot was emphatic as she said quietly, "Carol, that really does seem like a dangerous thing to do. What were you thinking?"

Carol looked around at all of them. "I let myself stop thinking and worrying and trying to control everything. I sat there, drinking this amazing wine and eating this incredible cheese, with my mind telling me all the reasons that I shouldn't be there, and my heart telling me all the reasons that I should. It felt so right to be sitting there with him. He is warm, and kind, and he makes me feel so beautiful and... desirable." Her voice broke. "I haven't felt any of those feelings for such a long time. And it felt so good." Her voice strengthened. "He is a sensitive, intelligent, lovely man. We went to his apartment, and we shared an incredible intimate experience that I will cherish for the rest of my life."

There was silence as everyone took in her words. Sophie was the first to speak.

"*You* are a married woman. I know life has been tough for you lately, but it doesn't change that fact." Her disapproving look indicated very clearly her opinion of the whole situation.

"I know. Don't you think I had all those same thoughts as I sat there with him? But... my whole life, I have been the good girl, the girl that helps everybody else solve their problems. Suddenly I just wanted the day to be about me, and Jean-Michel seemed to be the one to help me solve my problems, at least for an afternoon."

Amy looked at Sophie and her voice was hard. "Sophie, this weekend we've all seen that your automatic response is to see everything in black and white. Yet we've also had discussions about your situation with Roger where you now find yourself in a gray zone, right?" Sophie nodded somewhat reluctantly, and Amy continued. "Carol's situation is not black and white either. It's complicated. And there's a real possibility that someone, or several someones, will get hurt. It's going to be hard to resolve. But set all of that aside for a moment. Paris has offered Carol a unique chance to step away for a moment from her real life and her problems. It's offered her the chance to put herself first, which we all know she *never* does. I think that's a good thing."

Sophie still looked disapproving. She turned back to Carol. "Are you going to tell George?"

"I don't know." Carol sighed. "You've made the decision that you want to know whether Roger has had an affair, and also that you still want to make your marriage work. If I file for divorce, which is the direction I'm headed, it seems to me that it would just be hurtful to him, a last slap in the face, to tell him about this."

There was a thoughtful silence before Sophie spoke again, quietly. "I know that I do tend to jump too quickly to what I'm sure is the 'right' answer. In this case, I want to understand your side of it, Carol. I don't like what you've done, from a basic moral perspective, but I need to be more open-minded." She paused. "Can we talk more about this over dinner, after I've thought more about it?"

Carol shook her head. "I understand your feelings and your reaction to this. But this was my decision. I honestly don't want to talk about it or Jean-Michel any more."

Margot went over and turned on some soft music. "Why don't we leave it at that, then? Let's reconvene and start cooking in an hour or so?" With nods, everyone went off in separate directions.

When Sophie heard Margot head to the kitchen forty-five minutes later, she went to join her. "What can I do?"

"Well, the champagne is chilling and the pasta water is boiling. We just need to put a salad together while I get out the tomatoes, mozzarella, and fresh basil. Oh, and there's asparagus to steam."

Amy wandered in. "Looks like things are under control. Do you need help?"

"We need wine to have with dinner. You want to go to the *cave* with me?"

"Sure."

They headed down the stairs and Margot turned to Amy as she unlocked the *cave* door. "Hey, I just wanted to say that you can always ask if you need money. I know it's been tough for you, and

Paul and I are doing okay." She went on. "I guess I'm the only one in a two-income household... at least for another couple of months." They looked at each other and laughed.

Amy nodded. "Thanks for the offer. And don't worry about your situation. You'll find a great new job."

"Thanks, I know there will be opportunities and I'll figure it out. I just wanted to let you know that I'll always do what I can for you."

"I know." Amy smiled and gave her a quick hug.

Upstairs once more, they re-entered the apartment and Margot said, "Let's get that champagne open!" Amy opened the bottle with a resounding pop and, as she was pouring glasses for everyone, Carol rounded the corner. "What did I just hear?"

All four stood hip-to-hip in the tiny kitchen. Looking around, Amy said, "We have re-found each other this weekend. Let's toast to staying found." All four clinked glasses.

Carol said, "I'd like to propose a toast to Mom. I can't believe it's taken me all weekend to think of it. After all, it was her illness that brought us back together. Can we call her after dinner?"

Margot nodded, adding, "We need to do this again—and bring her with us!"

All four clinked glasses again. Margot laughed, saying, "Though we'll be pretty crowded! Who's going to sleep on the couch?"

Carol surprised them all by saying, "I know a great place to sleep."

Amy laughed. "I think this afternoon has done wonders for you!" She gave Carol a big hug.

They all moved into the living room, where they quickly polished off the pasta salad, green salad, and asparagus.

Amy marveled, "Josh and I try to eat healthy food at home, but it's so different here! With that great market and the great butcher shop, everything here seems fresher, more natural."

Margot spoke up. "Time for cheese. Anybody have room?"

All nodded, though Carol said, "I would never have believed I could eat so much. I bet I've gained five pounds in five days."

Margot shook her head. "I think you'll be surprised. I always feel like I eat more here, but then with all the walking, I don't seem to gain anything."

"I hope you're right." Carol got up. "I'll bring the cheese plate. Do we need more bread? A little? Okay, I'll be right back."

She went to the kitchen and they could hear her humming as she put the cheeses on a plate and cut more bread.

Amy turned to Margot and Sophie and spoke softly. "I know what she did seems crazy, but listen to her out there. She really sounds happy."

Sophie looked sheepish. "I think Carol's learned how to 'live in the moment.' And I've learned that I am too quick to judge." She was cut off from speaking further as Carol returned with the cheese arranged beautifully on a plate, and the basket of bread under one arm.

"*Voila!*" She looked at Margot. "How was that? Give me a couple more months and I'll be speaking like a native."

Margot looked mischievous. "Well, actually, depending on who you spend that couple of months with...."

Carol blushed and laughed. "Stop that! That isn't what I meant and you know it!"

Everyone laughed as Amy refilled the wine glasses. She looked at Carol and spoke quietly. "Carol, you deserve to be happy. And we are all behind you. I just wanted you to know that. Right, Sophie?"

Everyone looked at Sophie, who reached over to grab Carol's hand and squeeze it. "I have to be honest and say I still don't really like what you did, but Amy and Margot are right. I need to let that be your decision. And I haven't seen you this happy all week."

Amy added, "Who knows? Maybe some more Jean-Michel time might be just what the doctor ordered."

Carol blushed again and looked around at everyone, eyes brimming. "Thank you all for being supportive. I've thought a lot about what happened, and I do not regret anything. In fact, just the opposite. I'm going to try to stay in touch with him." She paused. "These five days have reminded me that everyday life can feel fun and relaxed. I honestly had no idea how tense my life had become at home. I knew that I always had to choose my words carefully in conversations with George to avoid getting him angry, but now I see how bizarre some of his other behavior is. Like when he throws his little hissy fits and walks out on us for hours at a time. I assumed that was normal—that everyone did that." She put up a hand to stop Amy's outburst, and continued. "I know it's ridiculous to you that anything like that could seem like it's normal. But don't you see? It *is* normal for him." She searched for the right words. "And then spending time with Jean-Michel, and feeling so relaxed and happy with him, even for such a short time, it's clear to me that in life there should be more fun and relaxation. I know I can't escape to a different world like that all the time—I'm not that naïve. But it's obvious that I need to make some changes in my life, at home and at work."

Sophie spoke quietly. "From your stories, it sounds like it's the moment for more drastic action." She added, "And I want you to know that I think it's the right decision."

Carol nodded, then turned to Amy. "What do you think? You're the one person here who has already gone through this."

Amy was silent several moments then spoke slowly. "Divorce is devastating. No one gets married believing they'll end up in a courtroom. But I have to agree with Sophie. It kills me to see you hurting so much. And when I step back from my feelings and try to be objective, I still see way more negatives to staying with George than positives. The biggest negative is the gambling problem. There's no possibility of financial security with someone like that."

"Frankly, the only reason to stay together is if you honestly think it's better for the kids and, at this point, listening to the stress, I don't think it is. I mean, try to imagine what they are seeing and feeling. Lots of tension and secrets between the two of you, and a father who doesn't work, which can't be a good influence on them. They know things aren't right. I bet they've forgotten too what it's like to have a relaxed atmosphere at home."

Carol nodded. "That's a big reason for my decision. I don't want my kids to have all bad memories of their childhood home, memories of everyone tiptoeing around each other. That just isn't the way it should be."

Margot now spoke up. "I agree. I can tell you that Mark's behavior has created that sort of stressful, tense atmosphere at our house. No one wants a house full of shouting and anger. I don't like what it seems to be doing to all of us, and particularly to my other son. Carl has become very quiet and spends a lot of time in his room—trying to escape it all. It's been extremely difficult, and I have literally felt like I've had to shut down my heart to survive the hurt." She paused and took a deep breath. Looking at Carol, she said, "I honestly don't know how you've lived with your situation as long as you have. I couldn't have done it."

Carol reached over to grab Margot's hand. "That is exactly what I have done, shut down my heart. I used that exact expression in one of my last conversations with George before I left for this trip. And shutting down my heart can't be healthy for me or for the kids, who need my heart wide open." She added, "I know now what the next steps in this have to be."

Amy reached over and took Carol's other hand, and with her other hand, grabbed for Sophie.

Sophie, in turn, reached over and took Margot's other hand. The four sat, linked together, feeling the energy and emotion flowing through them. After several minutes, Carol broke free, wiping her eyes, and smiling through the tears. "I love you all so much. Thank you."

Margot took a deep breath. "Whew! This was supposed to be a fun celebration dinner before we head home. We need to lighten things up. Who wants ice cream?"

Amy stood and laughed, grabbing plates to take to the kitchen. "You don't have to ask me twice!"

Margot pulled ice cream cones from the freezer. "I picked these up the other day at the grocery, in secret. They're kind of like King Cones at home-- except smaller. The French don't do junk food the way we do."

"They look fabulous!" Amy said. "But what about these dishes?"

"Leave them. It'll be quick work to toss stuff in the dishwasher after we have our ice cream."

"I'd like to propose a toast," said Amy, holding up her ice cream cone. "To the three of you—all together, you are the perfect sounding board: Sophie, the logical one; Carol, the emotional one; and Margot, the cheerleader!"

Everyone threw pillows at her. Then Margot started giggling, and it soon became obvious that she couldn't stop. Just like in high school, once one started, it was impossible for the others not to be affected, and they were soon all holding their sides and wiping away tears. Margot glanced over at the clock, wiping her eyes.

"Oh my gosh, it's eleven o'clock! Has everyone finished packing?"

"Not me!" said Amy.

"Me neither," said Carol.

"Then Sophie and I will clean the kitchen," said Margot. "You two get going!"

****

The next morning was filled with last-minute chores: showering, stripping the beds, and making sandwiches for the trip. By 9:15 a.m. they were standing in the hallway, having a last look around.

Amy sighed. "I have loved being here, Margot. This is a great place."

"Thanks. I am *so* glad I had a chance to share it with you all." She looked at her sisters earnestly. "I know it was not just expensive, but a long distance to come and a long time to be away. That said, I really hope we can figure out a way to do it again! And not too far in the future." There were nods all around.

Carol opened the door, rolled her bag into the hallway, and pushed the elevator button.

"Since I'm first, I will be riding with the bags," she announced with a big grin.

"Well, Ms. Shy gets a backbone!" Amy laughed. "I'm okay with the going down part anyway, so no argument from me."

They rattled their way across the cobblestones and out the giant door to the street.

"I swear, my 'one' suitcase is ten pounds heavier," said Amy.

"I should have left more space when I packed!" exclaimed Sophie.

Soon they were on their way to the airport, bulging bags successfully stuffed into the trunk of the taxi. The slight drizzle outside the windows matched their mood, as their thoughts turned inward and each started thinking about being home again and the serious situations to be faced. An hour later, they were getting out of the taxi, grabbing bags, and heading into the terminal.

Margot led the way to the American Airlines desk, and turned to face everyone. "This is where I drop you all off. I'm United, so I'm further around the terminal." She was silent, and everyone felt the pressure of too much to say and no more time to say it. They each took turns silently hugging Margot, before getting into the line that snaked around the corner toward the check-in desk.

"*Bon voyage*," Margot said. With a small, tear-filled smile, she continued on her way, waving once before moving out of sight in the crowd.

Amy was the first to speak. "What a great trip."

Carol nodded. "Definitely. Though 'great' doesn't begin to describe what we've experienced in the last five days, you know? The walking, the shopping, the amazing food—and, most importantly, the re-connecting. I not only re-connected with you all, but also with myself."

Sophie nodded. "How can so much have happened and yet it feels like we just got here?"

They lapsed into silence as each thought about what lay ahead. After checking in, there was time for a quick stop for duty-free chocolate and wine, and then they headed to the gates.

"This is where we split up," said Carol. "Sophie, I got Amy on the way over and you get her on the return!" All three looked at each other, and Carol gave each of the others a quick hug before setting off for her gate. "Keep in touch, okay?"

Sophie and Amy made it to their gate and settled in to wait. Pulling out the first of their sandwiches, they spontaneously toasted Margot for her foresight.

"Margot was right. I'm starved already," said Amy through a mouthful of bread and cheese.

Sophie added, "I'm glad to have these tastes as my last meal in France."

It was time to get back to life as usual. All four knew there were discussions to have, and decisions to make. The issues that had weighed so heavily on them individually before the trip were now less burdensome, supported by invisible threads of love and encouragement. They all felt the relief of sharing their burdens. No one could predict what the final results would be, but they all hoped there would be a chance to share those results in person. Soon. In some fun meeting place. That was a goal that they could *all* work toward.

They had been reminded of the importance of a support network made up of people who know everything about you and still love you. Of people who will take on the burden of your problems as their own, who will offer a sympathetic ear and sometimes a solution, and who will always share stories of their own. People who are there for you, no matter what. That's what sisters are all about.

The End

ABOUT THE AUTHOR

Marty Almquist lives with her husband in Arlington, Virginia. She has two grown sons and an everlasting love for Paris, where this, and future novels, will take place. Her blog, *I'd Rather Be in Paris*, is at www.martyalmquist.com.

Made in the USA
Lexington, KY
20 December 2014